SOLASTA

THE HIGHLANDER FAE

Nita Lynn Lipan

To my amazing hubby for always being my number one fan and cheerleader; who always saw my capabilities when I could not; and for supporting all my crazy ideas. This one's for you babe.

"Whatever our souls are made of, his and mine are the same."

–Emily Brontë

CHAPTER 1

Escape

A NIGHTMARE—NO, a premonition—woke Maximus from his sleep. He instantly sat up and then froze. Jada, sleeping soundly next to him, was startled awake. "What is the matter?"

When he did not respond, she knew something was wrong. To share in his vision, she placed her hands on his chest, linking herself to him. They both began to cry as a vision unraveled before them.

The future, if not changed …

"The Kelpie Ring! We must make it to the Kelpie Ring." The Ailey sisters ran from their burning home as the dark fae hunted them. Their brothers and father attempted to hold the fae off to allow the women to escape. The first to fall was their patriarch, Maximus. As he moved to stop one of Stygian's minions, another lanced him from the side.

River, the eldest Ailey son, roared with fury. Using his ability to fly, he was able to deflect the onslaught and kill the minion who slayed his father. Rune and Ronan combined their powers of strength and weather to create a tempest to block the dark fae from the few survivors. They miscalculated Stygian's powers. Their tempest halted and threw them across the village square. Rune fell to his death and Ronan was gravely injured. The Ailey women gathered their powers to save their youngest brother.

Celeste used her ability to create illusions to blind Stygian. She was able to hold the enchantment for a moment to allow Aurora to use the Earth to pull Ronan from Stygian's grasp. Once he was freed, the remaining Ailey family members ran for the Kelpie Ring.

The premonition began to fade into the darkness, releasing its oracle.

Ever since Stygian became the Fae King, Solasta transformed from a luminous and wondrous realm to a stagnant pit filled with hate. Each fae village slowly became discontented, villagers blaming each other for the King's rampages. Their once-vibrant colors faded into a doldrum array of grays and blacks. Stygian wanted war and vengeance against the mortal realm. He needed the strength of the strongest fae families to break the barrier.

He first attempted to bribe the families with wealth and land but soon learned that they would not comply with his machinations. Stygian resorted to controlling the masses via fear. The fae families did not know when or where they would be attacked if they did not do as the Fae King asked. Members of their families would go missing; others would be found on display in the village square with their ears mutilated and tied to a scaffold.

The female fae suffered a fate worse than death if they turned away Stygian's advances or demands. The unfortunate soul would be stripped, placed on display, and whipped. He would steal her beauty by shaving her long, beautiful hair, leaving her bald. The final blow would be the removal of her powers, placing them within a crystal to add to his collection.

As Stygian collected these crystals, his powers grew. He realized if he could steal the powers of the ancient fae families, he would not need the fairies to attain his vengeance. He would be the all-powerful and mighty Stygian, conquering all the realms. He would reward the fae who joined his cause and gifted them crystals to strengthen their own powers. This was when the days of the Ailey family were numbered.

Jada released her connection with Maximus as the premonition faded into darkness. "The fates have been kind and sent us a warning. We can change the outcome for our village; nothing is set until the first act has happened. We now have the upper hand, Maximus."

"Yes, my love, we will save our family and village."

The oldest of the fae families, the Ailey's, were the strongest of all the bloodlines and knowledgeable of the ancient ways. When they combined their powers, no one could stop them until Stygian came to power. They were a family of eight, truly a sight to behold. Their three beautiful daughters had raven hair, violet eyes, and slight frames with delicate features. The three brothers were similar with their violet eyes but had hulking frames modeled after the Greek gods. The family was a force. Each child inherited a magical talent from their parents. Celeste, the eldest daughter, could read the minds of others and manipulate their thoughts. Aurora had the power of the elements, earth, air, fire, and water. The youngest daughter, Brianna, could bring you back from the brink of death with her power to heal.

Their parents, Jada and Maximus, both had the gift of sight, always knowing what dangers lurked around the corner. The only limits the patriarch and matriarch had were that they could only see the future as it is being thought of. The outcome could change drastically until the first event took place. The Ailey brothers were blessed with powers as well. River had the ability of flight, Rune had Herculean strength, and Ronan, the youngest of the brothers, had the ability to control the weather.

They were prosperous. Their fellow villagers and tenants adored the Aileys. Crops flourished, animals thrived, and the village was joyful. They were the last stronghold left that defied the new Fae King. His world of vengeance and hate was not what Solasta was founded on. Their Elders embraced the circle of life, knowing there must always be balance between the good and evil of their world. Now the balance had shifted.

Their enchanted world began to unravel. The gloriously lush forests with babbling brooks and cool lakes became murky and muddy, no longer clear pools of purity. The Aileys knew they must intervene to save their people, family, and way of life. Maximus had lost so much in the last several years. His parents were murdered by Stygian, his brother Magnus betrayed the family, and the eldest Ailey brother was lost the day Stygian came to power. He would not allow more tragedy to come to his small village.

The Kelpie Ring was their only haven. Twice a year, the fae were able to travel between the fae and mortal world. Sentries were always posted during the equinoxes to assure no human would ever trespass into their realm. This would be their only way to escape Solasta and save the few fae that remained.

As Maximus rallied his fellow fae to coordinate a plan, a vision took hold of him once again. He saw mass destruction, the death of his family, his daughters taken as slaves for the Dark Fae King. His sons hung and placed on display for all to see what lies before them if they continue to defy him. Maximus knew if he were to take the powers of his sons, wife, and himself, there would be no stopping him, and both worlds would be no more.

Jada sensed her husband's terror and placed her hands on his chest to share in the vision and calm his soul. She saw the flames, homes ablaze with families locked inside. A group of fae with their wings torn off and Stygian absorbing their powers with his many crystals. The horror overwhelmed her, and she broke the connection. "We must save the village," she said. "These acts have not happened yet. The plan must be set in motion now. The vernal equinox is a sennight away; we can make the preparations and create the illusions for safe passage. The sentries will need to be enchanted; Celeste is strong enough. She can blind them or alter their vision to see what we wish."

Maximus, in his stoic manner, understood the gravity of their plight and knew they needed to take action now. With a week to accomplish their escape, many plans needed to be arranged. *Who would escape with them, where would they go, how would they get there, and once in the mortal world, how do they close the Kelpie Ring to stop Stygian from following?*

The night before their escape, the Ailey family ensured all preparations were complete. They had stores of food, tools, clothing, and tapestries. Their village of Luminia was prepared to flourish in the mortal realm. They enjoyed a last meal together. Spoke of memories and stories from long ago. Drank elven wine made from pomegranates and ate delicious pastries with meat pies. To help protect them from harm, the patriarch of the family diminished his powers to the point of nonexistence to create a special amulet for each of his children, along with a small, intricately designed box made of ebony. Each son had a signet ring set with a ruby and a different band. The gold signet ring was for River, symbolizing the sun, the titanium for Rune, to reflect his strength, and the silver for Ronan, to mimic the silvery gray sky before a storm.

If the rings were placed together and made into one, whoever wore it would have the powers of all three brothers.

Singularly, the ring would enhance the power of the owner. The only way for the rings to work was if someone from the bloodline of the Ailey family were to wear it. No one else could unlock its power.

For his daughters, he fashioned beautiful necklaces with different gemstones encircled with diamonds and hung on delicate gold chains. Celeste's was set with a sapphire, Aurora's with a golden topaz, and Brianna's with an emerald. Just like their brothers, their amulets enhanced their individual powers. When the amulets combined, they formed a Tulip, which signified perfection and royalty and allowed them to share their powers as one.

Maximus thought of everything to assure their family magic would never fall into the hands of the Fae King. In the devastating thought that one of his children were to be murdered, their amulets would absorb their power and re-appear attached to the next sibling's amulet. This would guarantee the amulets would not fall into the wrong hands. Maximus then presented River with a mysterious gift. As the eldest son, he would be the next patriarch of the Ailey family. "My dear boy, this parcel is to stay with you at all times. Never open it. Whenever the time may come and I no longer am with you, it will provide answers that you desire." River looked confused as he accepted the wrapped package. "Remember, River, do not unwrap the parcel until you are already in the mortal realm. If you are not able to maintain it, assure that an Ailey family member has it in their care." River nodded and accepted the cryptic command.

As the dinner was coming to an end, each parent presented their gifts to the children. Jada, who was a prodigious seamstress, created delicately embroidered handkerchiefs that could camouflage small items for each son. For her daughters, she designed an elaborate shawl that would magically tell the story of the Fae people, their family, and their village. As their final talisman against the coming evil, each child received a small, hand carved box holding a bit of earth from their small village. "No matter what may come, Luminia will always be alive within this soil," Maximus told his children.

Each child received their gifts somberly knowing these were their last moments as a happy family and they would endure many trials before they would be reunited. To lighten the mood, Celeste told everyone to hold hands and create a circle. "For us to succeed," Celeste explained, "we must not ponder on what is to come but relish in the new and the many possibilities that await us." She joined the circle and began to imagine the world she wanted for her family.

"Everyone close your eyes." Celeste began to imagine a beautiful, lush forest, green as emeralds. Through the forest ran a small stream filled with fish, otters, and other wildlife. They played in harmony, and if you listened quietly enough you could hear the river sprites singing their beautiful song beckoning any weary traveler to come for a cool drink. As the images began to fill everyone's minds, Celeste began to add a small cottage, followed by a field set with rows of pomegranate, almond, and apple trees. There was a pen for livestock with chickens, goats, and cows. They would be at peace, and the Kelpie Ring would be reopened for all to cross. "What a beautiful vision, my dear Celeste. Thank you for the gift of hope." Maximus embraced his daughter as tears ran down his cheeks.

The next morning all was set; the family ate a hearty breakfast and made their final preparations. The villagers were ready to depart. The plan was for the villagers to periodically leave the village and meet at the healing pools by the Kelpie Ring. They were to feign happiness, simply having a gathering to enjoy the new tulip blooms and picnic. This would be an easy task as the Kelpie Ring was the last location left with life. Each passing day the darkness crept closer to the Ring. The last family to leave the village would be the Aileys, except for Celeste, who would be at the Kelpie Ring to ensure the sentries were occupied.

As the families began to arrive and mingle in the healing pools, the sentries became suspicious. Knowing that today was the vernal equinox, the Kelpie Ring was open to fae for travel. To assure the sentries there was no plan or ill will, the villagers plied them with wine and food. They did not realize as they enjoyed their meals a few of the fae would disappear into the hidden cave near the entrance of the Kelpie Ring. Not every fae could leave Solasta. The elderly fae continued the illusion and would disguise themselves as the escaping villagers.

Back at the village, all seemed well until Stygian appeared with an entourage expecting a welcoming committee. He knew the Ailey family to be the oldest and most powerful of the fae. His plan was to marry Celeste, create enough heirs to guarantee his reign, and then dispose of her. Their bloodlines would become one.

The Ailey family was not prepared for the king's arrival. Celeste was at the Kelpie Ring keeping the sentries entertained and controlling their minds. As the Fae King probed the village, he noticed the lack of villagers. Stygian knew something was afoot. He sent his minions to begin to check the cottages. One after another, the homes were found empty, with personal effects gone. Maximus heard the commotion and realized Stygian knew that the village was escaping into the mortal realm.

Only Celeste was at the Kelpie Ring; everyone else was preparing the incantations to seal the ring to prevent Stygian from crossing and destroying the humans. "We must act quickly," Maximus told his family. "Stygian is here. We have been revealed. Hurry, everyone run to the Kelpie Ring." The family began to rush and complete their charms hoping to escape the demonic Fae King. He was grotesque, covered with boils and warts. Once a handsome fae with striking features, jet black hair and stormy gray eyes, the darkness took over his soul and his outer appearance began to mirror the evil that had taken root.

To add to the sickening sight, he wore his trophy of crystals that held all of the fairies' powers he had stolen as punishment for their disobedience. Maximus' powers were almost nonexistent due to making the amulets. It would be months before they would be able to rejuvenate. He had to send Celeste a message. Using the remnants of his powers,

Maximus used blood magic to send a message to Celeste to hasten the fae's departure, for now their plans were compromised. Stygian was on the warpath.

The Ailey brothers combined their powers of strength to control the weather. They created a maelstrom to slow down Stygian's progress. Jada and the girls ran to the Kelpie Ring. The sentries finally succumbed to the sleeping potion the villagers had placed in the wine, allowing the fairies to escape through the portal. As the families crossed, they immediately dispersed in different directions. Once the women were secured, Rune and Ronan began to make their escape to the Kelpie Ring to join the rest of their family. Maximus told the boys to not worry about him but to protect the women and children.

No one knew that Maximus had used the majority of his powers to create their amulets and would not be able to make the journey to the mortal realm. Before his eldest son, River, left, Maximus handed him an additional small parcel. He gave his son one last embrace and beckoned him to hurry. River knew this was the last he would ever see of his father and understood he was now the new patriarch of the Ailey family.

Moments before Stygian arrived, River made his escape. Maximus stood in his home as a King in his castle and faced the Fae King. Stygian's stench pervaded the cottage as his minions approached the Ailey Patriarch. "Where are they?" Stygian barked.

With his quick wit, Maximus replied, "Our beloved King, thank you for gracing us with your presence. We are honored to be visited by the Fae King. May I ask who you are referring to?" As Maximus spoke, the entire Ailey family began to walk into the cottage to greet the Fae King. Unbeknownst to Maximus, the moment Celeste received his message, she began to focus her magic on their home. She projected her family surrounding her father.

Stygian was stunned to see the entire family appear. "And here I thought your family evaded me. Even though I see you in front of me, I know how cunning your family can be. Achlys, go to the Kelpie Ring and assure all is well." The dark fae did as Stygian asked.

"My King, how you wound me. Our family would never dare to defy you." Maximus' words were meant to soothe the king with their cloying smoothness. Maximus hoped he had given his family enough time to escape. The Ailey family was assisting the last of the Luminian villagers through the Ring when the dark fairies arrived. Aurora created a wall of water to stop them, while her brothers continued to move the villagers through the Ring. Brianna awaited them on the other side to heal those in need. Arrows began to fly through the wall of water. Ronan attempted to help his sister and created a maelstrom to fight the dark fae. Unfortunately, the dark fae were true in their targets. As Brianna passed back through the Kelpie Ring to assist her family, she saw the torrent of arrows land their marks. Her brothers faltered to the ground, writhing in pain. They yelled for her to go and save herself, but she could not. Aurora saw what her sister was attempting and began deflecting the arrows off course with the wind while she maintained the water wall separating them from their enemies.

Brianna reached her brothers and began to manipulate the arrows out of their bodies. One by one, she removed the deadly objects and began to heal each wound. Her hands glowing and beads of sweat forming on her forehead, she hurried from one brother to the next. They were not at full strength, but strong enough to move and run toward the Ring to make their escape. Aurora was beginning to weaken, the water wall was weakening as well, allowing for the sentries to begin to make their way through.

Everyone was almost out. Celeste could not move, as she was still holding the illusion for her father back at their cottage. River knew if they did not all leave now, they would be captured, and the mortal world would be destroyed. He beckoned Celeste to break the illusion and leave, but she could not leave her father without protection at the mercy of the Dark Fae King. Tears welled in her eyes as she knew she must leave. "Celeste!" River yelled. "We must go and seal the Kelpie Ring!" They were the last to move through the passage.

"Hurry, everyone, place your charms around the Ring," yelled River. Immediately the Luminian families did as the eldest Ailey brother commanded. Each charm attached to the portal. The charms began to illuminate and electrify. The sentries made it past the wall of water, followed by their arrows. Their shadows were now visible from the mortal realm. The brothers began to fight the fae back into Solasta until the final charms and incantations were made. Once everything was in place, the brothers jumped away from the Ring. The portal to Solasta exploded with a light so bright, anyone who dared to see it would have been blinded.

The stones and dust began to settle, and the Kelpie Ring was no more. Their father was lost to them for all eternity, and Stygian the Dark Fae King sealed from the mortal world. They were safe, there was peace, and all would be well...or so they thought.

CHAPTER 2

Happily Ever After

Inverness

FIVE YEARS HAD passed since the Ailey family and villagers from Luminia made their great escape into the Scottish Highlands. For the first few years, they were in constant fear of Stygian breaking the barrier they'd created and the enchantments failing them. They roamed the Scottish landscape until they found a home. Inverness became their haven, and they called it such. The gorgeous seaside beckoned to them with a magnificent castle in the distance and a thriving village. An idyllic place for them to settle among the mortals.

Ensuring they could keep their identities hidden, the fae concealed themselves with elaborate headdresses and long flowing gowns to hide their elven features. The Ailey family was once again prosperous. Haven village began to grow in riches. Settled a comfortable distance from Inverness, the fae people were allowed to use their gifts to create thriving crops, farmlands full of livestock, and cozy homes with outdoor shops set up to sell their wares and culinary treats. The small village soon became known for its textiles and cuisine. All travelers from around Scotland would stop at the unique village to sample the local delicacies and bring home trinkets for their families.

Haven was truly thriving and growing. Each year, the villagers held a festival to celebrate their escape and remember those they lost. They disguised their festivities as a fete to celebrate the vernal equinox. They opened their village to the surrounding communities, providing games, music, and entertainment. It was the event of the year. The fae took opportunities to showcase their talents and procure new business opportunities.

As the head family, the Aileys hosted the opening ceremony. Their home, nestled in the center of the village, was the perfect location for the opening feast. They had tents with rows of tables set for families to enjoy a communal meal and pomegranate wine. Outside the tents were torchlit pathways leading to each event for the locals to discover. Jada was meticulous in her endeavors. She wanted to make Maximus proud. It had been five years since she last saw her husband, five years since she felt his caress, five years since she said goodbye. Her children told her he was lost, but deep down in her soul she knew he was still alive. She would hold onto hope until the fates told her otherwise.

Solasta

Stygian was beyond enraged when he was deceived and the Luminian villagers were able to escape to the mortal realm via the Kelpie Ring. Celeste had given her father enough time to hold off Stygian and his minions before the portal was closed forever. He knew Maximus held the key to breaking the barrier. Even though he wanted to tear him limb from limb, he restrained himself. Maximus would die a most gruesome death once he uncovered how to remove the enchantment.

The enchantments were created by the different families of the village. The only way for the portal to be reopened from the mortal realm would be to have a family member from each bloodline present at the Kelpie Ring, creating a Celtic circle, speaking the following words: *From day to night mysterious sprites allow our worlds to reunite.* As the villagers participated in this ritual they were warned. If they were to ever betray the fae village and attempt to reopen the portal, their powers would be stripped from them and added to the Kelpie Ring's barrier to strengthen its hold.

Maximus knew of the failsafe. His main concern was Stygian discovering the key to the Kelpie Ring's magic. He knew the moment Stygian realized what happened he would be dead. Maximus was astonished that Stygian did not immediately murder him as he stood in front of the Dark Fae King. Ready for a noble death filled with torture and humiliation, Maximus was ready to meet his demise. He was not ready for Stygian to take him as a prisoner. The last five years had been horrific.

He was tortured, starved, and beaten. Never once did he betray his family and village. As the originator of the Kelpie Ring enchantment, he was the key to breaking it. With the last of his magic locked away in the ebony box he'd given to River, there was no way for Stygian to probe or take from the Ailey bloodline. "You filthy swine! I will pull your toenails out one by one. You will beg me for mercy and death. How do I break the enchantment on the Kelpie Ring?" Stygian was furious. Each day that passed, his beatings became more and more gruesome.

After the first year, Maximus became numb to the lashings. "You may tear my flesh, break my bones, and bring me to the brink of death. You will never know how to reopen the portal." Maximus would laugh in Stygian's face before the next blow would land. Maximus knew as long as no one on the other side attempted to break the barrier, he would be safe. Stygian did not know with Maximus' death the portal would be sealed for all eternity, as the enchantment required the originator of the spell to be in the fae world and the others to be in the mortal realm. Only he could travel between the realms under the current enchantment. One day the Kelpie Ring would be open to all, but until then only Maximus could cross the barrier.

The significance of the small parcel he'd given River so many years ago was the key to Solasta's survival. Only when his village was settled and at peace would the parcel begin to call to him. He then could make his escape. Stygian believed Maximus' powers were completely drained, but he knew the value of the Ailey blood. Until he could unlock the barrier, Maximus needed to stay alive. Stygian did not know that the depleted fae's magic would return one day with the success of the new village and the love his wife held for him.

Haven Village

Even though everyone thought her silly, Jada spoke to Maximus daily in her dreams. The small parcel he gave to River was placed on their mantle. Each day the family would speak to it and share their wishes and hopes. They never dared to open the package. Maximus was always mysterious, and his family knew better than to open the ebony box without instruction. It was their Pandora's box, and they did not know what it would unleash. They all believed Maximus was murdered by Stygian the day they left Solasta. Only Jada believed him to still be within the living world.

As Maximus hung in Stygian's dungeon, malnourished, dirty, and sodden, he began to hear the calling of his ebony box. It was a faint whisper in the beginning that grew into a thunderous roar. The ebony box had fulfilled its task to collect the happiness within his home and tie it to the earth within its confines. River was true to his word in assuring the parcel never left their family. Before the families escaped, the ebony box and the accompanying boxes of earth his children held were imbued with ancient blood magic. The power held within the box was Maximus' remaining magic. It would call only him and attempt to rejoin its master when they were safe and their village in the mortal realm was prosperous. It was time to return to his family. The vernal equinox was the height of the fae magic. Even though he did not have his magic, the dream world always broke the rules. It was the subconscious that could travel through time and space. With every fiber of his being, Maximus began to meditate and place himself in a sleep-like state to project his thoughts to his wife within the dream realm.

Haven

As Jada opened the Vernal Equinox festivities and began the formal dinner, she felt faint. Her heart was pounding, and her mind began to feel foggy. Brianna, noticing her mother's behavior, stepped next to her mother to sense if she needed healing. Her mother reassured her that all was well and that she was just fatigued from the preparations. Once the dinner was in full swing, she would retire for a short while. She did not want to miss the singers and performers. The guests were seated at elaborately decorated tables with ivy, flowers, and fresh fruit with cheeses overflowing serving trays.

The eldest daughters of each of the villagers came out to serve the attending guests. Wild boar, venison, and duck greeted the diners with aromas to tempt the gods. The pomegranate wine flowed easily, and all the revelers were entranced. Conversations were lively, and the jesters provided plenty of entertainment with their quick quips and silly movements. The festival was off to a great start, and Jada took this time to sneak away for a quick rest. The moment she placed her head on her pillow, she was transported to the dream world.

Maximus was standing in front of her. Afraid to be disappointed, she slowly reached out to see if he was real. As her hand reached for him, she felt his hand caress hers.

"How could this be? My Maximus, are you truly here with me?" They were floating among the stars in a deep embrace. She held him so tightly. Kissed him, kissed his hands, kissed his forehead, and once again his lips. She knew he was alive!

"My love, we do not have much time before Stygian knows what I am doing. Even though I am here, my physical body is in Solasta in a trance. He will discover my attempt to connect with my family via the dream realm. The parcel I gave River holds the key to my return. I placed the last of my magic within the ebony box."

Jada's eyes grew wide. "Now I understand why you instructed us to never open it. Your magic would have returned to you. Stygian then could have drained you of your powers to destroy the Kelpie Ring."

"Exactly, my love. We must hurry. I do not know how much time I have before my trance breaks," Maximus told her.

Jada listened intently to her husband as he explained what she must do to release him from Stygian's dungeon and bring him home. "This has to be done tonight while the veil between the worlds is thinnest. You must tell our children to form a Celtic Ring around the parcel. Jada, as my one true love, you must prick your finger and have a solitary drop of blood fall into the center ring of the parcel. This will activate the blood magic to the hidden portal. Every evening at nine, Stygian releases me from my bonds to test my magic. Each evening, he grows more and more angry that the Ailey magic is not his. Now that the parcel calls to me, my powers are strong enough to make the journey from our world to the mortal realm. My beloved, you have done well. The parcel only would have called to me if you and the children were safe and at peace. Our village must be beyond prosperous."

Jada cried with joy and longing. She could not wait to have Maximus once again by her side. She repeated the details to Maximus to assure she did not falter in her duty to him. "We create a Celtic Ring around the parcel. Place a single drop of my blood in the center. Then we repeat the following words:

"Two worlds divided. Two loves apart. We summon the fae Elders to stand with us. As we join hands and summon our father. As he moves from realm to realm, seal his path so no other can trespass."

"You are correct, my dearest beauty. Once the incantation is spoken, I will be transported from Solasta to your village. The Celtic Ring must stay intact, and no one can release their hold, as the magic was created by our family love and bond. Tonight at nine, assure the incantation is complete. I will be able then to follow the enchantment to you. If all works according to my plan, I will be with you, and Stygian will be sealed forever in Solasta."

What Maximus did not know was that even though his magic was blood magic, held with the bond of familial love and all that was pure; it was still corruptible. He did not know that this fateful encounter would lead to a crack in the barrier and provide an opportunity for the malevolent Stygian to cross into the mortal world.

Jada awoke suddenly from her slumber. She ran to the small parcel on the mantle and noticed it vibrating. If you listened hard enough, a faint melody played from the box summoning anyone to open it, as if a call from a siren. Maximus warned Jada to not open the parcel, for it would unleash magic so powerful that it would destroy the barrier and thwart his return. She summoned her children with haste to explain what had just transpired. Skeptical of their mother's vision, they did know their father would have planned for all scenarios.

He was the most powerful of the fae, transcending all others. To guarantee they were not disturbed, Celeste created a vision for all the revelers. They would not see the family walk into the woods and begin the preparations for their fathers' return. All was in place; the family drew their Celtic Ring and positioned the small parcel in the center. Jada pricked her finger on a rose and released one solitary ruby-colored droplet of blood onto the center of the box. The droplet began to follow the Celtic pattern carved into its lid. The box began to vibrate more violently than before and soon revealed a beautiful, intricate design that channeled the blood. The family created an outer circle and held hands as they repeated their fathers' words. As the family spoke the incantation, the parcel illuminated. The siren song became louder.

They held on tight to each other to assure the Ring was not broken. As the incantation was repeated, the force became stronger and stronger. They did not know what to expect or how they would know the spell had worked. The family continued until the song and light grew so intense that it created an earth-shattering blast that threw the family back. After a few moments, they arose. Jada was the first to see the dark figure in the center of the Ring, followed by River, then Brianna and the rest of the Ailey family.

The shock froze them in place. Did they release a demon? Was it Stygian? The figure moved and slowly lowered his hood to reveal his gaunt and bearded face. It was Maximus! The family rushed him and nearly knocked him over. This was happily ever after. The Ailey family was once again reunited. Maximus collected the small parcel and placed it in his pocket for safe keeping. To maintain the balance of the barrier, he must conceal the power of the box. It was a magical portal made of blood magic tied to his bloodline.

CHAPTER 3

Chance Encounter

HAVEN VILLAGE WAS a bustling business center. Everyone wanted to visit the famous village located near Inverness. The ruling Ailey family, loyal to the Laird of the Asheboro Clan, provided fine linens, exotic fruits, and plenty of pomegranate wine for the local villagers to enjoy. It was a grand mystery to the locals, as the village seemed to have grown overnight and always held an air of wonder and majesty. The daughters of the Ailey family were gorgeous, with many suitors pursuing them. The Ailey sons looked as if they were Greek gods. Many of the village girls were smitten. The two elder sisters, Celeste and Aurora, loved their village life and were soon married. Their powers were strategically used when necessary to provide for the Asheboro Clan. This allowed for "miracles" to bless the villagers. Haven Village was always held in high esteem in the Laird's eyes.

Soon the Ailey sisters began to grow their families and grandchildren blessed Maximus and Jada. There was always the underlying fear that the children would inherit their mothers' powers. As this began to be revealed, the family unraveled their history to their in-laws, explaining their escape, and how they came to be in the Scottish Highlands. In the beginning there was fear, but it soon dissipated as they saw how benevolent the people of the once-called Luminian Village—now Haven—were. No ill will had ever been taken against the surrounding villages. The Laird of Asheboro became one of the wealthiest Lairds of the Highlands, with overflowing coffers thanks to the mysterious village.

All was well. The families lived in peace and continued to prosper. The youngest of the siblings, Brianna, was a lively and adventurous 17 year old. Her powers of healing were the most sought-after by the village. She grew her own garden of herbs and flowers to create her poultices. Her dyes were renowned around the Highlands. Colors that were never seen before in the mortal world, now burst forth against the greens and browns of the highlands. Brianna wanted more than village life, however. She wanted to explore what was beyond the forest and meet new and interesting people. Her life was grand, and she did not want for anything, except for true love. She hoped one day to meet a dashing Laird who would sweep her off of her feet and take her on seaworthy adventures with the mist of the water kissing her cheeks and warning the sailors of the siren song.

As Brianna went on her weekly walk through a meadow of wildflowers, she carried a basket with a small picnic lunch and jars of salves, taking inventory of what she needed to find. Lavender was always in high demand as it was her cure for almost all ailments. From steadying a nervous mother to treating wounds, lavender was the ingredient of Brianna's signature ointment. She also collected heather, marigolds, dandelions, and, hidden in a small cove, her treasured roses. Not native to the highlands, Brianna was able to enchant the small cove to grow roses from deep crimson to pure white. These roses were the key to many of her healing salves for severe wounds that became infected. As she gathered her materials, Brianna enjoyed a cooling swim within the cove and ate her packed lunch. In the distance, she heard a group of men on a hunt. Hastily gathering her items, Brianna enchanted her hiding place and climbed up the hillside to see what the commotion was all about. A group from Clan Cedar-Kellen was traveling through the forest. They sounded as if they were enjoying themselves. A stag ran past the group and they jumped to attention. The group shifted from jovial chit chat to focused hunters.

Brianna became excited as she watched the men in pursuit, taut muscles with beads of sweat rolling down their chiseled chests. She was entranced by the lead hunter. He had fiery red hair and piercing blue eyes as if made from the coldest regions of the fae realm. They seemed to glow when the sun shone on them at the right angle. As the hunt continued and men began to unleash their arrows, Brianna became frantic for the stag but exhilarated at the same time. The hunt would be over soon and the men gone. They were so close to catching their prize! She watched with intense anticipation, not realizing she was holding her breath. Then a rogue arrow went wild and hit her muse. The fiery redhead roared with pain but did not stop his hunt. He unleashed his arrow and the stag fell to the ground as he slumped in his saddle.

Amazed at his strength and determination, Brianna was frozen on her perch watching everything unfold. Her parents warned her to never interact with people outside of their village or lands because of the local fear of the fae. Still, she could not ignore the handsome man who was wounded. His clansmen acted quickly. His was not a mortal wound but left untreated would fester and possibly cause death. He was lucky the arrow had missed his lungs and went through his shoulder. The men did not need to push the arrow through as it had made its way out the other side, but they needed to break the point off to be able to remove it. Brianna knew the moment they removed the arrow he would bleed profusely if they did not immediately stop the flow. She needed to act now. She ran from her perch toward the group of men with no fear for herself, only wanting to save the handsome hunter.

"Wait! Please, I'm a healer!" she screamed. The men did not realize they were not alone. Brianna was alluring and did not realize the danger she placed herself in running into the group of men. She continued to repeat "I'm a healer, I'm a healer!" The group parted like the red sea to allow her access to their fallen clansman. With meticulous hands, she inspected the wound and began to give orders to the group. "You! Grab my basket and remove the three jars wrapped in cloth; you there with the long braid go into the forest and collect as much moss as possible to stop the flow of blood once we pull out the arrow." She continued to give orders until she had all she needed. With a gentle touch, she guided the arrow out of the injured man's shoulder. He was in and out of consciousness from the blood loss but felt a gentle warmth that soothed his pain. Quietly, Brianna sang the healing song her mother taught her to amplify her powers.

"Ash to ash, dust to dust, may the light from our ancestors heal this being. Ash to ash, dust to dust, may those who receive this gift of life forever thank the fates for sparing their soul."

As she sang the small poem, the wound began to heal until it no longer appeared. Even though the injury seemed to be closed, there was still much internal healing needed. Careful not to reveal the results of her power, she placed her poultice and salves on the shoulder and gave instructions to the group on how to care for the injury. As a final step to secure her safety, she made a draught for the injured man to drink. This would lull him to a gentle slumber to allow for him to have safe passage to his keep and to prevent the men from wanting to check the wound. She provided a few extra supplies for them to take. As she provided instruction, she assured the men he would survive and would need a sennight to rest in bed to allow his internal injuries to heal. They were in awe of her abilities being such a young maiden.

As a show of their gratitude, the clansmen presented Brianna with their clan tartan and a beautiful brooch. Brianna was shocked, as this was not a typical gift to be given to a healer or any other who was not betrothed or family of the clan. What Brianna did not know was she had just saved the Laird of Cedar-Kellen.

"You are too generous. I cannot accept such grand gifts. The greatest gift is knowing I helped a Laird continue to lead his clan," Brianna told the group. She knew by the manner in which his men treated her that they were a clan of honor. The clan insisted her heroic efforts in saving their Laird needed to be repaid and would not accept her refusal. Brianna graciously accepted their gifts and told them they would always be welcome in her village if they were ever in need. Clan Cedar-Kellen had heard of the legendary Haven Village and their beautiful linens, jewelry, and famous pomegranate wine. Robert, the brother of the Laird, thanked Brianna for her invitation. The group parted ways and the men began their journey back to Castle Dalkeith. The keep was a three-day trip from Haven, and the men worried their Laird would not make the journey.

They followed Brianna's instructions to the letter and did not remove his bandages until they arrived home. Throughout the trip, they fed him the broth Brianna provided and added oils to his bandages to keep them fresh. The clansmen were astonished when their healer arrived and removed the coverings. His skin was renewed! Not one single scar; if it was not for the fact that they saw his injuries with their own eyes they would have thought Laird Cedar-Kellen had played a cruel joke on them. The mysterious maiden who came to their rescue had to have been a forest sprite coming to their aid. There was no other way to explain the Laird's miraculous recovery.

Laird Cedar-Kellen was still weak from the loss of blood and needed the healer's restoratives with a healthy meal of beef to replenish his strength. He remained confined to his bed for another week before the village healer allowed him to return to his normal duties and training. Laird Cedar-Kellen could not forget the beautiful vision he had of a young woman with raven hair and electrifying violet eyes. He did not remember much of the hunting trip after he was wounded. He could only remember slight glimpses of what she looked like. He recalled the touch of her small, delicate hands removing the arrow, followed by an emanating warmth. As he fell in and out of consciousness, he could only hear her melodious voice as she sang a strange poem and smell the overwhelming fragrance of roses. The scent was lovely and her voice was a siren song calling to him. He needed to find her, lose himself within her song and touch. Laird Cedar-Kellen would find his muse and marry her, for he was convinced she was his one and true love.

Once he was completely recovered, the Laird began to question his men, asking if they knew her name or which village she came from. The only information he was given was that the maiden had welcomed them to visit Haven Village but did not give a name. They told the Laird they repaid her generous efforts with a clan tartan and brooch, as she had saved their leader. Cameron knew as the Laird he must marry and the one he wanted was a young maiden from Haven Village.

Brianna ran all the way home after her encounter with the hunting party. She was flooded with a multitude of emotions. She felt exhilarated by the hunt, exhausted from the healing of the Laird, and frightened that they would discover who she was and come for her and her family. Once she arrived home, her parents knew something was afoot. Brianna was drained, and her family quickly began to prepare a restorative for her. They laid her on the bed and allowed her to rest before they began to barrage her with questions. Brianna recounted her adventure. She began with encountering the hunting party and how entranced she was by the lead hunter. Jada squeezed Maximus' hand, knowing he was broiling with anger. Brianna was not supposed to interact with others, not in their village or clan, and yet she ignored their warnings and may have placed their family in danger.

Brianna took a deep breath and steadied herself as she continued her tale. She assured her family she remained hidden and the group did not realize she was even watching. The hunt was exciting with the men in full chase and the buck bobbing and weaving through the forest like a nymph. Then in an instant a rogue arrow hit the lead hunter in the shoulder. Not an immediately fatal wound, but if not cared for would most definitely lead to his death. "I was not going to interfere, father, I swear! But the men were not thinking and were ready to pull the arrow from his shoulder without preparing to stop the bleeding or even having supplies to cleanse and wrap the wound."

Maximus could not contain his anger for much longer. He knew his daughter's nature. Brianna could not let any living being become ill or die knowing she could possibly save them with her gift if they were not at death's door. Brianna's gift did have a limitation. If she was too late to be called or the person had a mortal injury, she would not be able to save them. She could ease their passing, which took its toll on her. For her 17 years she had witnessed too many deaths, and her family shielded her whenever they could. Brianna understood the balance between life and death. She respected it and would not interfere if she knew there was no hope. As her story continued, Brianna explained how she'd run out to the group. Everyone in the room held their breath knowing how dangerous her actions were. She reassured them the men never touched her or hurt her in any way. There was a collective sigh as they heard her words.

Once the group realized she was there to help, they allowed her to approach the wounded hunter. As her mother taught her, she hid her power by masking it with poultices and salves explaining to her family how she ordered the group to retrieve the necessary items. Once she was able to heal the hunter, she provided the clansmen with a small staple of supplies and a sleeping draft to keep the hunter calm for their journey. Now for the end of her tale. Brianna took a cleansing breath to steady her nerves. She grabbed her collecting basket. With trepidation, she removed the beautiful clan tartan and brooch the men had given her as payment for her healing efforts.

Maximus roared with anger when he saw the gifts. "No! This cannot be! These men cannot know who we are. They will come for us and hunt for you." Brianna tried to reassure Maximus.

"Father all is well, no one knows of my powers or who I am." There was no way to calm Maximus. Jada knew his temper. Attempting to bring him back to a place of subtle calm, she placed her hands on his heart to share in his emotions.

"Maximus, our daughter did a noble deed. She healed a clansman that could one day become an ally." Jada was able to bring Maximus back to a tolerable level after several minutes and a few broken items.

Brianna was allowed to complete her story. "Believe me, father, I tried to return the gifts, but the clansmen would not allow it, for I did not know I had saved the Laird of Cedar-Kellen."

"One question, Brianna", said Maximus through clenched teeth. "Did you place a memory draft in their wine to forget about the encounter?" Brianna's eyes went wide as she realized her grave mistake and quietly answered her father.

"No". If it was not for the enchantments placed on their home, the entire village would have crumbled under Maximus' fury as the earth began to shake the very foundation, all would have been turned to rubble.

CHAPTER 4

The Invitation

WEEKS HAD PASSED since Brianna's chance encounter with clan Cedar-Kellen. Her fathers' fury dissipated in time and he once again was his loving and stoic self. The Ailey family began to return to their daily routine of hunting and gathering, tending their farm lands, and venturing out to the forest. They began to lose the fear of discovery and possibly coming upon the unknown clan once again. Clan Cedar - Kellen had never ventured as far as Haven Village, but the small bustling village was now well known for their goods. No one could pass up the chance of visiting the famous location, sampling their delicious pomegranate wine and pastries.

To assure the family's safety and that of the village, the community placed additional protective charms that would alert the heads of the households of any unwelcome intruders. If a newcomer were to ask for a maiden healer, the villagers were to immediately alert Maximus. Brianna was to be placed in hiding until the newcomer had completed their business or left the village via a distraction from the villagers. Brianna did not enjoy this portion of her new routine.

She did not see any harm in meeting the new clan or them visiting the village. Her father was adamant that they must stay hidden, for if they were discovered it could lead to total destruction of their new home and the possibility of the Kelpie Ring reopening, in turn allowing Stygian to escape his current prison in Solasta.

Each time she would question her father he would repeat the same words, "Brianna, I love you. I love our family and the life we have built. We cannot throw away all we have done and accomplished by placing families in danger due to a girlish fancy for an unknown clan."

As a dutiful daughter she would reply, "Yes father, I understand." It killed Maximus seeing his wildflower being restrained when she was meant to roam free, but he had to think of the family and of their village.

Brianna having such a grand adventure on her last herb collecting day was no longer permitted to collect her herbs alone. A member from her family had to accompany her on any of her trips to her enchanted cove. Brianna loved her family dearly and did not mind her new entourage when she would leave for her expeditions. She did miss the quiet solitude she once had to daydream, swim in the cooling pools, and simply breath away her daily musings and stress. As the village healer, Brianna to some extent controlled life and death. She felt every pang of pain someone felt.

After a day's healing, she would be physically and

mentally depleted.

There were days the healing was so exhausting she would not rise from her bed for hours or even days. She was highly sought after, and the Laird of Asheboro adored her. She had saved his queen from certain death after she had her last child. Both mother and child survived the harrowing birth. Brianna was given a bejeweled box as a token of their appreciation for saving them. In addition, she was given the honor of a betrothal to the future Laird of Asheboro, Braun. Not wanting to offend the Laird, Brianna thanked him for his generosity. Gently she told him she could not accept such a gracious gift, as the finest gift she could have ever received was the health and wellness of the Queen and her new bairn.

Laird Asheboro was astounded by Brianna's maturity and grace. He would not accept refusal of his bejeweled gift but allowed Brianna to step down from the betrothal; she was only 15 at the time and Braun was 20. The Laird would not give up so easily, however. Brianna was a beauty, the daughter of the wealthiest family within his lands, and the village healer; she was a prize to have and adore. He did not know of the family's magical ties, but he did know he wanted to maintain the wealth and prosperity within his lands.

From the day Brianna turned 16, the Laird of Asheboro met with Maximus to propose the betrothal of their children. Maximus with his wisdom always rallied for his youngest daughter. He explained the choice alone was up to Brianna to accept a marriage proposal. Only the truest love would be good enough for his youngest daughter. He would not allow mortal traditions to dictate her future. His two elder daughters did not have adventurous, fiery hearts. They enjoyed the quiet village life and raising their families.

Brianna was different. She longed for adventure, for more than this provincial life. She wanted to heal others but be part of a grander mission. Her father understood her, yet her mother did not. Jada wanted Brianna to be safe, secure, and not want for anything. Braun possessed these things and would provide the security Jada wanted for her youngest daughter.

Braun did try to court Brianna. He was the ever-doting admirer. He loved Brianna for her beauty and nothing more. The sight of her healing others made his stomach turn. He loved her dedication to the village but did not care for her wants and desires. Braun shared many family dinners with the Aileys in hopes of gaining favor with Maximus and Brianna. To no avail—Brianna was headstrong, and Braun made her skin crawl. There was a darkness that surrounded his aura. She would not accept the match.

"Brianna, please. Accept Braun's proposal. This will secure your future."

"I will not accept his offer," Brianna retorted. Each conversation Jada would attempt to address the proposal resulted in an angry confrontation leading to Brianna storming away into the woods. Maximus knew he had to resolve this issue amicably. He was still at the mercy of the Laird. Both the Laird and Maximus were level-headed men. After much discussion, the men came to terms that their children would not create the union their families so wished. Laird Asheboro, having a daughter of his own, understood Maximus' stance. No one would ever be good enough for his princess but if she were to choose a lucky clansman to be her betrothed he would allow it, knowing his daughter would select a good man.

Nevertheless, the Ailey family and Asheboro Clan would forever be aligned, with the gracious Laird accepting the mysterious people of the woods onto his lands and earning their respect and trust. The fae in turn earned the Laird's favor when Brianna saved their Queen and young bairn. With disappointed ambitions, the patriarchs let the matter go. Unbeknownst to the families, Braun had other plans, and he would not surrender so easily.

As the days grew warmer, Haven village continued to grow in popularity. The festival of the Vernal Equinox would be upon them soon. This year, the Laird wanted to throw the festivities and invite Haven Village to the keep along with their closest clans from the Highlands. Laird Asheboro wanted to thank Haven Village for their continued support and prosperity. He also wanted to divert Braun's obsession of Brianna toward other suitable maidens from the neighboring clans. Perhaps they would be able to find a grand match for Braun and align Clan Cedar-Kellen with the wealthy Asheboro clan.

Learning of the Laird's dissolution of the betrothal with Brianna, Braun fell into a melancholy state. No one was able to pull him from his dark and pensive mood. When he saw Brianna in the village, it took every fiber of his being not to pounce on her and take her for his own. She would smile at him and speak as if they were the best of friends not knowing the thoughts that were constantly running through his mind. Braun was clever and charming; he would woo Brianna and would not accept her refusal to marry. "She will change her mind once she realizes what a catch I am," he would say to himself.

Braun was truly delusional; he did not realize that Brianna wanted more than a physical attraction. She wanted an adoring husband who would support her endeavors, have long conversations on philosophical thoughts, and would see her for more than her beauty and the future children she would one day have. Braun wanted to possess her as his own, for she was the most beautiful maiden in their lands. He played a good game of admiring her as a healer and showing interest. These were all tactics to win her over. The moment she would become his, he would not allow her out of his sight. There would need to be a new healer in their village for she would no longer be part of the daily village life. She would be in the keep bearing his children and concerning herself with their upbringing.

As Braun obsessed over Brianna, his thoughts became darker, and soon his impulses were becoming more difficult to control. He would find himself watching her from a distance. Anytime she would drop an item, he would run and collect it to add to his shrine to her. The Ailey family did not know soon there would be an enemy among them and Brianna's life would be in mortal danger.

The fete was three days away and Laird Asheboro heard from all the clans accepting his invitation. This would be a festival to end all others. No cost was spared and the prosperous Haven Village provided the most amazing delicacies and entertainment. The Ailey family was invited as honored guests to join Laird Asheboro and his family at their banquet table. The villagers could not refuse such an honor. Even though they feared discovery, it was more important to maintain their clan ties with Laird Asheboro.

The Haven villagers prepared their finest attire with silks and jewels. If anyone were to see them they would say the King of England would be shamed by their regal appearance. Asheboro keep was all a buzz with the preparations. The Laird urged his son to participate in the arrangements, hoping to draw him out of his sulking mood. "Braun, there will be hundreds of beautiful maidens attending our fete this year. Perhaps you will find one you will admire and pine for as you did with Brianna. Do not linger in the past, for you will miss the life that lies before you. Brianna has made her choice. Both her father and I respect her decision, and so should you. You will be the future Laird. Find peace in this storm and focus on what awaits you on the other side. Search for a maiden that is kind, loving, beautiful, and capable at the fete. The union of two such individuals will continue to strengthen the Asheboro clan."

Braun did not hear a single word his father said, as he was fixated on the image of Brianna in the distance helping a young child with a scraped knee. How he wished for her hands to touch him and caress his every ache. "Braun! Did you hear me?"

"Of course, Father. I will seek a match at the fete and leave the past behind me."

"It will become easier, Braun, I promise. A first love is difficult to lose, but time will heal the wound." Laird Asheboro hoped Braun took his words to heart but was still concerned his son was in a dark emotional place.

Braun could no longer contain his anger and acknowledge Brianna would not be his. He needed an escape. Braun decided to go on a hunt to relieve his tensions. He gathered a small group of men to form a hunting party. He explained to his father he would return the day of the fete and assist in any preparations but he needed time away from the village and Brianna. Laird Asheboro understood and gave his blessings.

The group left two days before the fete. Braun decided he wanted to explore a new hunting area. Perhaps it would be a fruitful adventure. As they wandered through the untraveled path in the woods, Braun noticed the foliage did not seem to grow like the woods by Asheboro keep. The trees looked gnarled and petrified as if they were dead. At closer inspection, the trees were alive but oozing an onyx-colored sap. The leaves were a dark green with black veins pulsing. Braun and his men had never seen such a sight.

As they moved further into the woods a strange mist began to appear around them.

The men realized it was coming from a pool with crystal clear waters that held dazzling diamonds, emeralds, and rubies at its edges. "It's the Kelpie Ring," one of the men said.

"It cannot be, it is a myth, a simple legend," said another in the party.

Braun did not know what they were speaking of. "What is the Kelpie Ring?" he asked. His best friend, Logan, came to tell the tale of the mysterious Ring that allowed mortals to walk among the fae.

"Weary travelers would drink from its pool and awake in another realm not knowing how they had arrived. Others said they would walk through the Ring created by the water and the bridge crossing it entering a place called Solasta. Mortals were always welcomed until one day there was a Laird who wanted to take Solasta for his own using the fae for their many talents and riches. He stormed the Kelpie Ring with an army. As the army entered the new realm, they began to take the women and children for their own evil pleasures. The men were tortured and slaughtered as if mere animals with no dignity. The Solastians did not have a chance to defend themselves. They had never experienced such ill will from the mortal realm. As the fae began to gather their forces, half of the realm was destroyed. The Laird was a fierce warrior and greed was his driving force. The Elders of the Solastian realm gathered their powers and decimated the army. Legend says only one man was allowed to survive, for he did not participate in the attack, a young bagpiper who wanted to see the action. He was told no mortal would ever return to Solasta. If they were ever to return, they would suffer a fate worse than death. The young lad was returned to the mortal realm and an enchantment was placed on the Ring, sealing the portal forever." Braun was entranced by the fairytale and wondered whatever happened to the people of Solasta and the Laird's keep when he did not return.

"Let us move on," shouted one of the men in the hunting party.

"We do not want a wisp to guide us to our demise," stated another. The pool and its bridge did not seem welcoming. There was a feeling of a beast lying in wait to pounce on its prey. Braun ignored his men's wishes. He looked at his clansmen and laughed. "Are you young bairns still on your mothers teat? Pansies, the lot of you, if you believe in the wisps. There is no such thing. We will take a moment to enjoy these cooling waters and then continue our hunt." Perhaps if he could find a gem so precious and perfect to give to Brianna she would change her mind and marry him.

Logan spoke to Braun and tried his best to convince him not to swim in the waters. Braun was too consumed with the thought of the beautiful gems and finding a treasure to win over Brianna. Unbeknownst to the group, Stygian was lying in wait beyond the Kelpie Ring. One of the cruel jokes of the Ring was the ability to see the mortal realm but not be able to enter it. The Kelpie Ring was strong, but it had a small fissure that allowed Stygian's dark magic to seep through.

As unwitting travelers would find the Ring, Stygian was able to lure them to the pool. Upon entering the pool, their minds would be corrupted, driven mad with thoughts of evil fae torturing them. Eventually they would succumb to their mental hysteria and kill themselves, ending their torment. As each man would release his soul, Stygian would collect it to add to his enchantments in hopes of being able to break the barrier and enter the mortal realm. Something was different about this mortal. He spoke of a maiden named Brianna. He had not heard this name in several years. Could it be the youngest daughter of Maximus? Before tormenting this mortal he would probe his mind and see if there was more to his story. Perhaps he could use him.

Braun dove into the cool waters of the pool. The water was refreshing and tranquil. Swimming for a short time, he saw a radiant gem sparkling beneath the surface. It was unlike any other he had seen before. The gem was a gorgeous aquamarine color as if plucked from the ocean with specks of gold throughout. This was the gem he would bring back to Brianna. *I will fashion it into a beautiful bracelet to adorn Brianna's delicate wrist*, he thought to himself. As Braun dove to acquire the gem, it seemed as if it moved farther away the nearer he swam to it. Braun was beginning to lose his breath and thought it best to return to the surface.

Suddenly something grabbed his leg. Braun struggled to break free, but the more he struggled the stronger the hold became from his unseen enemy. He continued to kick in an attempt to swim away. The invisible assailant pulled him further into the depths of the Kelpie Ring. Braun regretted his decision to swim in the pool, forgiving Logan for his actions and not heeding his words. He questioned his every decision, *Why did you jump into the pool, you idiot? For a maiden who does not even care for you and never will.* Numerous thoughts continued to run through Braun's mind as he began to lose consciousness. *I will die a fool and no one will ever know how much I truly love Brianna.* There was no hope as Braun could not see his men and in turn they could not hear his pleas for help. Darkness then took over.

CHAPTER 5

The Pact

BRAUN WAITED FOR the pain of death to consume him. He waited for the convulsions to begin due to the lack of oxygen and the water to begin filling his lungs. Perhaps the fates would have mercy on his soul and allow him to die peacefully. A calm began to envelop him as he thought to himself, *At least I will no longer pine for my sweet Brianna and obsess over her beautiful face, long flowing raven hair, piercing violet eyes.* Braun waited, and waited, and waited, but the pain never came. A slow ethereal glow began to appear and spread warmth throughout his body. He opened his eyes and before him there was a floating mist engulfing him in the waters. He was not able to move but had a sense of comfort and well-being.

A voice began to speak to him. "Hello, curious traveler. Why have you entered my waters?" Braun attempted to respond but could not make a sound. He began to panic, not knowing if the being would harm him. Braun's thoughts began to race. He thought of his father, his family, the keep,

Brianna's beautiful face and the men on the shore. The voice once again began to speak. "Do not be frightened, curious traveler. Your keep is safe as are your men and family." Realizing the being was reading his thoughts, Braun calmed himself. He knew he was still under the cool waters of the pool but he was able to breath with ease. Slowly Braun began to collect his thoughts hoping to be released from this magical mist.

"Who are you? Can you help me get back to my hunting party? I only wanted a gem for a maiden I wish to marry." Question after question he continued to give but there was no reply. Braun once again began to lose hope. As his eyes closed to allow death to take him the voice returned.

"For a curious traveler to dive into a pool for a gem you give up very easily." Braun, wanting to simply die in peace, wished for the voice to go away.

"I know not who or what you are but let me be. I have nothing left?" The mist began to form into a shape continuing to move in wisps around him. He then began to recognize a figure emerging of a beautiful watery fairy with silver blond hair and eyes the color of icy glaciers. She reached out to Braun and began to sing.

"Sabrina fair,

Listen where thou art sitting

Under the glassy, cool, translucent wave,

In twisted braids of lilies knitting

The loose train of thy amber-dropping hair;

Listen for dear honor's sake,

Goddess of the silver lake,

Listen and save!"

Could it be the legend of the water sprite who saves men from a fate worse than death? Braun asked himself. The fairy continued to move closer and gently caressed Braun's face. *Tell me your secrets, curious traveler, and I will grant your heart's desire.* Braun knew for sure he was dying if not already dead. This mythical being was an Aphrodite. Perfect in every way. She simply requested his secrets to have his heart's desire. *What does it matter?* He thought he was going to die at any moment once the waters began to fill his lungs.

He told the story of his lost obsession, of the beautiful maiden with raven hair and violet eyes. "She is the village healer who consumes my every thought. From the moment I saw her I wanted her. She does not want me. I tried everything to win her love and affections but I am not her match. I was hoping to collect the gem for her and recount my adventure in retrieving it. Perhaps my bravery would win her over and she would be mine. My precious, my treasure, my love, oh Brianna," he lamented.

The sprite looked intrigued. "Tell me more of this Brianna. Does she have other suitors or perhaps a family?" Braun did not know that the mysterious water sprite was an illusion created by Stygian, the Dark Fae King. He was playing with a wolf in sheep's clothing.

Preying on weary travelers for two years, Stygian would consume their souls in hopes of growing stronger. Each day, he grew uglier and more disgusting. He reeked of rotting flesh mixed with a pungent aroma that would make anyone faint instantly. He needed to leave Solasta and destroy the mortal world. He needed to avenge his family's murders once and for all. Stygian did not know on this fateful day that a link to his former subjects would so unwittingly fall into his hands. He was careful to not kill this mortal. As Stygian continued his ruse, he began to discover where the Village of Luminia had settled. They were now in Haven Village under the protection of Laird Asheboro. Braun continued to divulge the history of this new village and its prosperity within the community.

Stygian grew hungrier for more information but knew this mortal would not last much longer in the trance he was placed in. Soon the spell would end and he would drown. "Curious traveler, what is your name?"

"I'm Braun, son of the Laird of Asheboro."

"Young future Laird, you have piqued my interests and I will save you for this maiden you love so dear. Here is your gem to take, but before I save you and return you to your men, you must make a blood pact that will seal your promise to me."

"As you wish, water sprite."

"When you return to your village, say nothing of our meeting. As you visit Haven Village, return to me every week. Tell me tales of the village, their people, and families. I may ask for small trinkets as the time passes so that I may learn of your ways."

Braun felt this was a simple request and perhaps each time he returned he would be able to attain a new gem to bring to Brianna. The sprite produced a small blade puncturing Braun above his heart. A droplet of blood released from his chest. It began to bead and swirl around in the water turning into a dark red ruby. The sprite collected the new gem and placed it into her hair as if it were a barnacle to be implanted into her being. In return, the Sprite produced the aquamarine gem Braun so desperately wanted. The moment the gem touched Braun's hand, the waters began to swirl, creating a whirlpool encompassing his body. As the whirlpool grew stronger it began to raise Braun to the surface.

His men were waiting for him, thinking his soul was lost. Once his face broke the surface they all began to scream and cheer that the future Laird survived the mysterious Kelpie Ring. Braun raised his hand to reveal the beautiful gem. He showed the men his prize. As they gazed upon it, the gem looked alive as it pulsed and glowed. The flecks of gold shimmered, illuminating the stone as if wild lightning bugs lived within it.

Braun was a legend. No one had ever returned from the Kelpie Ring. Even if they did return, they came back as different men, crazed with delusions, and eventually succumbed to their shattered minds. Braun seemed to be invigorated and emboldened, now possessing the gorgeous gem. His men asked him what happened, and he simply replied, "Sabrina Fair" and nothing more. He dared not break his promise to the water sprite. He was not sure if breaking his blood oath would cause great harm to himself or family.

The hunting party began their return to the keep and were blessed by the forest nymphs with a multitude of venison and pheasant for the vernal equinox feast. Braun and his men presented their gifts for the feast to Laird Asheboro and were greatly rewarded for their efforts. Each hunter in the party received a beautiful brooch and clan tartan to wear to the banquet. They were also invited to have the honored seats next to the Laird and his family. The group of men left the keep to prepare and bathe for the upcoming fete.

These next three days would be filled with joy, laughter, and hopefully love. Braun hurried to prepare for the feast. He wanted to find Brianna to present her with his prize and once again ask for her hand. He had already had a golden bracelet made; it was just missing the perfect stone. Now that he had the gem he could set it in place and win her heart.

Once the bracelet was complete, Braun rushed to leave the keep and find the Ailey family. He tried to steady his heart as he walked up their cobbled pathway to the front door. As if knowing he was arriving, Jada opened the door and welcomed Braun. "What brings you here, Braun?" she asked. "We were just about to leave to join the celebration of the equinox."

"Lady Ailey, I have come to present a gift to Brianna and hope to ask for her hand." Jada was stunned; she knew Maximus and the Laird dismissed any notion of Brianna marrying Braun.

Jada, wanting to be gentle, furrowed her brows and asked curiously, "Has Brianna changed her mind since last we spoke?" She knew well enough that Brianna wanted nothing to do with Braun.

"No," Braun replied, "but I believe once she hears of my heroic action and sees the glorious gift I have procured for her she will change her mind." Jada understood now. Braun was truly enamored with her daughter and thought that she could be easily swayed by feats of strength and trinkets.

She was of the earth, wind, and fire. Nothing could contain Brianna's spirit. She did not want to be the Lady of the Keep in Asheboro. She wanted adventure and a new land. Braun was more of a brother. He never took interest in her other than for her beauty. They did not share the love of reading or playing chess. She loved her garden, herbs, and patients. Braun loved himself and did not care about diplomacy. His father was a great man and leader. His son still had much to learn before becoming Laird.

When Brianna spoke with Braun it was always about his achievements, never about her wants and needs. Jada tried to stall as much as possible, but it was becoming late and the family must leave so as to not offend the Laird of Asheboro.

She searched for Brianna and Maximus to assure all would go over smoothly.

Brianna emerged from her room in a beautiful lilac gown that made her raven hair and violet eyes stand out as a magical siren call. Her hair was plaited in an elaborate design with a golden circlet atop it. Her slim waist was encircled by a golden girdle. The fabric fell along her body, embracing every curve. As an added embellishment to her hair, Brianna had pinned the brooch from Clan Cedar-Kellen among her ringlets. Braun could hardly contain himself. He wanted to take her then and there. His self-control was truly waning the longer he had to wait to possess her.

He pulled out a small velvet pouch to show Brianna and her parents. He opened it to reveal the beautiful contents. It was an intricately designed bracelet of gold, a Celtic ring design intertwined with leaves of ivy. In the center lay the gem he recovered from the Kelpie Ring. Braun reached for her hand and slid the bracelet onto her wrist. With his zealous excitement, he somehow scratched Brianna with the ornate bauble. A small ruby red droplet of blood appeared on her wrist. He apologized as she removed the item from her hand, smearing the drop onto the gem. Brianna was growing exasperated with Braun's antics.

"Braun, we are friends, and I love you as my brother, nothing more. I long for the ocean, the hunt, and adventure to new lands. I want more than a village life. You will one day find your true match, and she will be the luckiest woman alive to have you as her husband. Please know I cannot marry you but respect you and wish the very best for your future life."

Braun could not believe what he was hearing. She did not even want to hear how he attained the gem. The hours he spent forging the bracelet. He was inflamed. His body felt hot as if it were burning with fever ready to instantly combust. "I see," Braun stated with clenched teeth. The Ailey family knew they were in deep waters. They needed to navigate the situation carefully. Brianna could see Braun's body tensing with anger. "Please Braun, let us not part this way. We have always been friends and enjoyed many family meals together." No longer wanting to seem a fool, Braun became abrupt.

"I thank you for your time my lady, but I must take my leave." Braun turned, wrapping the bracelet back into its velvet pouch, exiting the Ailey home for the last time. *She will be my wife whether she is willing or not,* he thought to himself as he stormed off.

CHAPTER 6

Love at First Sight

THE AILEY FAMILY was slightly shaken after their encounter with Braun but hoped he would cool off before they arrived at the keep for the opening banquet feast. Jada calmly soothed Brianna and cleansed her arm from the smeared blood. As she was doing this, a vision came to Jada. She froze in place and began to weep. Maximus, sensing Jada's distress, came to her and shared in her vision. As the husband and wife embraced, the vision began to emerge, blurs of faces began to appear, Brianna in danger, Braun leading a war party, the gem from the bracelet appeared and was placed in the Kelpie Ring with her blood still on it. The Kelpie Ring began glowing and then darkness. What was happening? How could the Ring be activated? Jada and Maximus broke their embrace.

They could not hide their emotions. They knew Stygian was coming and somehow Braun would be the person to break the barrier, allowing for his dark destruction to come into the mortal realm. How were they supposed to warn the Laird of the impending danger and the role his son would play?

"We can still change this," Maximus stated. "These events are based on the emotions of Braun now. We will need to follow him closely and see what transpires. We will go into the feast and play our parts. If it is possible, I will speak with Laird Asheboro to see if I can persuade him of the danger Braun may create. Braun is angry and immature. He does not know what he has engaged with. If he has been altered by Stygian in some way, we are all in grave danger. We first must retrieve the bracelet. If Braun learns of the true nature of the Kelpie Ring, he can unleash Stygian by collecting all of the family's bloodlines and placing their gems into the Ring. He already has our family blood. What will he do to attain the others?"

As the family began their walk to the keep, Brianna could not contain her nerves. "All will be well my child," Maximus soothed his youngest. As they reached the keep, the rest of the Ailey siblings joined their parents and youngest sister. They were a handsome collection of fae. The villagers were in complete awe of them. No one in Asheboro knew of their history. Only the families of Celeste and Aurora were privy to knowing that fae lived among them. Tonight they may need to reveal their origins to protect themselves and the mortal realm.

The family took a collective breath to steady themselves before entering the grand banquet hall. It smelled of warm spices with tables upon tables of fruits, cheeses, and wines for the revelers to enjoy. Laird Asheboro greeted his honored guests and sat them to his left to join his family. The hunting party was also honored and brought to the right of the Laird's family to be seated. The guests made their way into the hall and sat at their tables. Brianna, still not feeling herself, needed a moment and excused herself. Her mother wanted to follow but decided that Brianna just needed a moment of fresh air to wash away the day's events before playing her part at the feast.

As she left the table, someone grabbed her arm. She was alarmed as to who would dare touch her in such a manner. It was Braun. Her body tensed, and she tried to pull away from him without making a scene. He had a sadistic look on his face and attempted to hide his malice with a sly smile. "Brianna, forgive my behavior earlier today. I was upset, I did not handle the situation well. I see that we will solely be friends. May I ask your forgiveness and honor me with wearing the bracelet I fashioned for you. It will only be a symbol of our friendship and nothing more."

Brianna knew from her mother's vision that they needed the bracelet back. Hesitantly, she acquiesced to Braun's gesture and took the small velvet pouch the bracelet was held in. To assure him of her forgiveness, she gently opened the pouch, slipping on the bracelet. Not wanting to be rude by leaving his side, Brianna excused herself from his presence. She proceeded to walk through the hall to a side entrance where she could escape for a moment.

As she walked through the doorway to the outdoors, she realized she had found the herb garden, beautiful and fragrant. She could smell the soothing scent of lavender with the invigorating scent of kumquats. She found a small bench and sat with her eyes closed, enjoying the solitude. Brianna was unaware that Cameron, the Laird of Cedar-Kellen, had witnessed the events leading to her sitting outside alone. Initially he thought the young maiden was in danger when the host's son grabbed her. She looked as if she were a trapped animal needing a way to escape. Cameron began to move toward them, as no one else seemed to see the young woman's distress. He could not hear what was being said but noticed the maiden with the raven hair begin to calm as the future Laird removed his grasp.

There was an exchange, and the maiden took the gift. It was simply a lovers' spat and now all things were settled as they parted ways. Something still gnawed at Cameron about the maiden. There was a familiarity about her, as if he had met her before. He did not want to start a brawl over a maiden who is betrothed to the future Laird, but he needed to know more about her. He followed her to the gardens, watching as she sat and closed her eyes to enjoy her fragrant surroundings. She looked as if she were a goddess among her subjects. As the daylight began to fade, Cameron could see a solitary tear run down her delicate cheek and wondered what would bring her such sadness.

She looked at her wrist, removing the bracelet that was given to her and placed it once again in its pouch. "May the fates bring someone for Braun so he will let me be," she spoke. As the maiden prepared to return to the banquet hall, Cameron saw his mother's tartan brooch in her hair. *Could it be? Was this the young woman who saved my life consuming my every dream and thought?* Not wanting to frighten her, he made a slight cough to announce his presence. Brianna startled, looking up at the handsome hunter she had saved so many weeks ago. She did not know he'd been invited to the equinox festivities. Her breath became shallow and her hands clammy.

This was her hunter, her adventurer, her nightly dream of passionate kisses and soft caresses. Her heart's desire was standing in front of her, and she did not want to be found alone with him. "Perhaps we should move indoors where you can be chaperoned." Cameron realized the significance of their meeting and did not want to taint the moment with vulgarity from the keep. He entered the hall first and assured no one was looking.

He signaled to Brianna the all clear and she returned to the hall. Once in view of all the keep, Cameron walked up to Brianna and bowed. "May I introduce myself, milady?" Seeing this new interaction, Maximus came to Brianna's side to assure proper etiquette was followed. At that moment, everyone, including Braun, turned to the couple in the center of the room.

"Milady, my name is Laird Cedar-Kellen. I am in your humble debt, for you saved my life two moons ago. My men were gracious enough to gift you the beautiful brooch you wear this evening as payment for your services. I have yet to repay my debt personally." Heat rose to Brianna's cheeks as the Laird gently picked up her hand and placed a kiss upon it. The moment his hand touched hers she was on fire. Her body did not feel as if it were hers. She had imagined this moment so many times and how they would meet. She never thought it would actually come true. Her heart began to race, and she did not know if she would be able to contain herself. His lips were a whisper above her skin. If it were possible, she would have melted instantly into his hands.

"My Laird, you have no debt. I was very thankful I could be of service to you and your men. The gifts your men bestowed upon me that fateful day were extravagant but they would not brook my refusal."

"Good men," he stated. "Would you honor me this evening with the first three dances of the feast?"

"If it so pleases you, my Laird." Brianna was giddy with anticipation for the feast to begin. Laird Asheboro was intrigued by the couple and their chance meeting.

"Regale us, Laird Cedar-Kellen, of the heroism our dear Lady Brianna performed to deserve such a grand gesture of admiration."

Cameron began his tale, painting the most picturesque images for a stag hunt. "We were in hot pursuit of a glorious stag. Its antlers were the largest I had ever seen, at least 18 point. This would truly be our prize if we were able to capture such a virile and agile creature. I had the animal in my sights and was ready to unleash my arrow. Then a rogue arrow struck me in the shoulder." Cameron continued to tell his story and draw the revelers into the heat of the tale, with a brave young maiden running toward a group of men to help a wounded man she did not know. "She risked her life, virtue, and reputation for a mere stranger. I owe her my life. I am honored that she would wear my mother's brooch this evening. Her beauty surpasses any ornament man can create."

Brianna blushed with his compliments. The Ailey family was honored by the Laird of Cedar-Kellen. Maximus invited Cameron to join them at the banquet table to learn more of this man who was so enamored with his daughter.

By this point, Braun was incensed. If he could kill with his thoughts, the Laird would have fallen dead where he stood immediately. How dare he speak to his future wife and shower her with such attention? Braun's mood grew darker as the evening passed, watching the Laird of Cedar-Kellen interact with the Ailey family.

He noticed when Brianna would laugh and joke with the Laird. He imagined himself by her side rather than Laird Cedar-Kellen; each time she touched his shoulder or blessed the Laird with a smile drove a dagger deeper into Braun's heart.

As the evening continued, Brianna danced every dance with Cameron. She could not stay away from his touch. They shared in conversation and learned that they both loved the epic poem, Beowulf. Brianna began to recite her favorite quote from the poem and Cameron joined her in completing it.

"No, we two in dark of night shall forego the sword, if he dares to seek war

without weapon, and then may wise God, the holy Lord, judge which side will

I succeed, which one will win glory, as to him seems right."

She was astonished by the Laird's interests and sense of adventure. This was the man she wanted to spend her days with, this was the man her dreams were consumed by, even though it was too soon to marry, she knew one day this man would be hers.

As the feast began to end and the revelers slowly left to retire to their lodgings, Brianna and Cameron continued to be engrossed in conversation. Finally, Maximus interrupted the lovebirds and excused his daughter from the Laird. "Until tomorrow, Laird Cedar-Kellen. Will you be competing in the games?" asked Maximus.

"Aye, of course. I will be in the hammer throw and Caber Toss," responded Cameron.

"Then, my dear Laird, I will be watching with anticipation of your success." Brianna gave him a seductive smile and a gentle curtsey before leaving with her father.

Highland Games

The second day of the equinox festival was buzzing with excitement as maidens dressed in their most beautiful attire to impress the clan men competing in the day's events.

Brianna could not contain her joy as she prepared her basket of herbs and donned her favorite frock that was shimmered in hues of blue with gold accents. She knew the day's events would bring injured men to visit her tent, and she wanted to assure all the materials she needed were available.

The first event of the fete was the Caber Toss, men in kilts straining to toss a caber to land at perfect 12 o'clock. Clan MacGregor always took the prize of honey and bread each year, as no one could ever beat them. *Perhaps this year will be different,* Brianna thought to herself. Once all of her items were packed, Brianna made her journey to the keep with her parents to prepare their tent. They always offered water, sweet pomegranate wine, and an assortment of fruits from their orchard to the game attendees.

Everyone was in good spirits as they prepared for the day. Cushions with blankets were laid out for the women to watch in comfort while the children roamed the different activities provided by the numerous vendors. The Laird of Asheboro truly did not spare any expense when creating the three-day fete. Whiskey was plentiful, food never ending, and the company was more than entertaining. The Ailey family was ready to view the Caber Toss when Braun approached the trio.

"Good morning, Braun," Maximus greeted. "Will you be competing this year?"

Braun, still agitated from the previous evening's events, was abrupt in his reply. "It is my duty to represent my clan as the future Laird. I will be competing in the three main events of Caber Toss, Hammer Throw, and Archery." Brianna's face could not hide her astonishment and joy.

"Wonderful, Braun," she said. "Laird Cedar-Kellen will be competing as well. I will make sure to cheer for you both." Braun gave Brianna a condescending glance.

"As if you care," was his reply.

Brianna understood his pride was hurt. Braun was simply acting out of anger but there was something that nagged at Brianna. She could not place her finger on it but she knew that something was afoot. Asheboro Keep was alive with all of its visiting guests. The crowds were gathering for the first event of the day. Braun, Cameron, and several other men were ready to take their turn at the Caber Toss. Ian from Clan MacGregor was the favored winner. They always had the fates on their side and won year after year. There were new contenders this year: Clan Jacobs, Clan McCallum, and Clan MacArthur to add to the competition. Laird Asheboro signaled the piper to begin the games. The melodious tones of the bagpipe rang throughout the competition field and the Clans began to cheer as their champions walked up to their positions to greet the Laird of the keep, while hoping to gain favors from the maidens in the crowd.

Brianna's heart was racing as she saw Laird Cedar-Kellen walk up and greet Laird Asheboro. Their eyes connected for a moment, causing Brianna to become instantly flustered. She felt as if her body was on fire and only the Laird could quench her thirst. She wanted to assure the

Laird his intentions were well received and produced a delicate handkerchief that she embroidered herself with his crest surrounded by roses. She walked up to the front of the crowd for Cedar-Kellen to notice her and held out her favor for him.

When he saw Brianna walk up, Cameron could not contain himself. Every fiber of his being pulsed with the urge to kiss her. He saw that she held something in her hand. As he approached Brianna, she took a few small steps forward. Brianna curtsied and presented her token to the Laird. "Dear Laird Cedar-Kellen, may this favor bring you luck and safety throughout the games today." Brianna smiled and under her breath said, "Do not kill yourself Laird, for who will I dance with this evening?"

"Such a statement from an innocent maiden?" he replied.

"Only for you, my Laird."

This small interaction gave Cameron all the strength he needed to toss the caber to the next realm. He was in another universe. Braun saw the couple together. Rage was beginning to blind him. *How dare she give him a token?* Once Cameron walked away, Braun walked over to Brianna with a disgusted look. "Will you cheer for me as well?"

Brianna, uncomfortable with Braun's closeness, took a step back and smiled. "Of course, Braun, you are my family friend. I would not wish any ill on you. May the fates be ever in your favor."

"May I have a token?" he asked. Brianna grew more uncomfortable with their interaction and searched the crowds for anyone to come to her aid. She did not want the clansmen to believe she was a flirt or anger Laird Cedar-Kellen.

"Braun, how you jest. My favor is with Laird Cedar-Kellen." This reply of course fueled the simmering anger Braun was attempting to control. He became more bold in his requests to Brianna.

"Well, then, if you have no favor, may I have a kiss for luck?" Braun pulled Brianna toward him to take what he wanted.

Brianna struggled to release herself from his grasp. She attempted to scream but Braun took that moment to kiss her. His hands gripped her so tightly he was beginning to bruise her skin. Instantly Brianna kicked at her assailant. This caused Braun to lose his grip, releasing Brianna. She quickly slapped Braun across the face.

"How dare you take such liberties!" she yelled, hoping the commotion would draw attention to them and bring her assistance.

At that moment Cameron turned to give Brianna one last bow, when he saw her struggling with Braun. No one was willing to interfere as he was the son of the Laird and thought it a lovers' spat. Cameron knew better. He ran toward the couple.

Attempting to control his own anger, Cameron gently removed Brianna from Braun. "May I be of assistance?" Cameron said to Braun.

"No, Laird Cedar-Kellen, I was just playing with Brianna."

"She did not seem to like the game you were playing."

"It was just a small kiss."

Cameron turned to Brianna seeing her violet eyes begin to well with tears and a bruise begin to form where Braun had grabbed her. "My dear Brianna, is this true?"

"No, Laird Cedar-Kellen. Braun asked for a kiss as a favor. When I refused, he grabbed me and stole a kiss." Cameron nearly lost his composure when he heard what the future Laird had done.

Braun shrugged it off and told Cameron, "You know young maidens; first they say yes and then when caught will say no."

"I do not know maidens in the way you speak of, Braun, and I suggest you keep your distance from my future bride!"

Stunned, Brianna looked at the Laird with awe. He'd only known her for a day and already felt as if she were his match! Braun was taken aback with Cameron's bold statement.

"How dare you propose to her? She is to be mine, and no other man will have her." His words were dark and menacing. Brianna was not going to cower in front of Braun, even though her legs were ready to give out at any moment.

"I will never marry you! I once thought we could be friends and move past this. I see now that this will never be. You are no longer welcome in our home. Our fathers may be friends, but I want nothing more than for you to never be in my presence ever again!"

Laird Asheboro could not see the commotion that was arising but knew there was something wrong. He stopped the piper and went over to the forming crowd. Laird Asheboro found Braun arguing with Cameron. Brianna was standing next to the Laird as if about to faint at any moment. The crowd spread apart as they saw Laird Asheboro approach. "What is the meaning of this?" he exclaimed. Braun began to speak, but the Laird quickly placed his hand in front of Braun and turned to Laird Cedar-Kellen to explain.

"Laird Asheboro, Braun accosted Brianna. He forced himself upon her and stole a kiss." Cameron turned to Brianna to assure he did not misspeak on her behalf.

"Is this true, Brianna, did my son accost you and no one in our village came to your aid?" Brianna shyly acknowledged Cameron's words.

"Yes, my Laird."

The Laird then turned to his son. "How dare you touch another without their consent? I have not raised a son who would abuse others. Have you ever seen me lay a hand on your mother with hate or intent to harm, have I mistreated our servants? Why would you ever think this would be an action I would condone?" Braun was speechless. He had never seen his father so angry in his entire life; even as a young boy he never raised a hand to him as he had seen others do. Laird Asheboro thanked Cameron for his bravery; he understood what it meant to confront a future Laird.

"But father, he has proposed to Brianna. Do I not have the right to claim what is mine?"

"Hear me now and hear me well Braun, Brianna is not a possession! She is a maid with a choice. She has chosen not to accept your offer of marriage. Her father and I have been friends and agreed that as unfortunate as the event was to us, she may choose to marry whoever she fancies. We have explained this to you, boy! I have witnessed enough of your dishonorable conduct. You have shamed your family and will not be competing in the games. Leave my sight, for if I hear of another incident with any person you will no longer be my son or the future Laird."

Both Brianna and Cameron were shocked at the Laird's words. Braun turned slowly and left the fete. He returned to his quarters in the keep and remained there for the rest of the evening.

Laird Asheboro turned now to the couple. "I hear that there is a proposal?" Brianna smiled and looked up to

Cameron; Cameron looked at her with pure joy. "This was not the intended form I wanted to share with everyone, but it is true, my Laird. I wish to marry Brianna. She saved my life and has bewitched me beyond saving. I cannot live a day without her, now that I have found my muse."

Laird Asheboro could feel the simple joy radiating from the pair. "You must first ask her father for her hand. If he agrees to the match, I will bless the union and announce the betrothal on the final evening of our festival," declared the Laird. "Now that all the excitement is over, let us continue with our games. May the favor of the fates be with all the champions." Laird Asheboro signaled for the piper to once again play to announce the contestants.

Cameron gently lifted Brianna's hand to his lips and asked, "May I?"

She acquiesced to his request. The whisper of a kiss sent an electric shock throughout her body, leaving her faint and wanting. Cameron left her side with a devilish smile and a promise of more to come.

CHAPTER 7

Meeting in the Woods

AFTER BEING DISMISSED by his father, Braun lost all rational thought. He was made a fool by Brianna, Cameron, and now his own father. He was tired of this game of cat and mouse with Brianna. *If she cannot be mine, then she will be no one's,* he thought. He stormed to his quarters and packed a small parcel of supplies, leaving enough room for food once he passed the kitchens. No one questioned Braun as he placed a bottle of mead with bread and cheese into his satchel. "I will visit my water sprite. She will help me," muttered Braun under his breath. The servants thought he surely was going mad as he continued to speak to himself. "I will ask the water sprite for vengeance. I will become Laird." Once he gathered all his supplies, Braun stormed from the kitchens and made his way to the Kelpie Ring.

The games were more entertaining this year than ever before. With new clans joining the games, once-known winners were sadly unseated and new champions rose to the top. Clan Cedar-Kellen won the Caber Toss, Archery, and Wrestling matches. Clan Macdowall won the dancing competitions and piping exhibitions. On the final day of the games, all the winning clans came together for the tug of war. Coins were being placed for the winning clan. Villagers shared their thoughts and questioned who would win. Would it be Clan Cedar-Kellen to unseat the reigning champions, Clan Jacobs? The bets were placed two to one for Clan Jacobs.

Laird Asheboro was excited to see the last two clans compete. This event would decide who won the golden chalice and the honor of marrying one of his daughters. Wanting his son to join the festivities, the Laird thought two days was enough time for Braun to have licked his wounds. His son always had a tendency to sulk for long periods of time. Even as a man, he had not outgrown this behavior.

Laird Asheboro was not regretful of his forcefulness; he wanted to assure Braun knew the gravity of his actions. As he approached his son's quarters, he noticed the door was open. The room looked as if he had not been in the keep for several days. He asked the scullery maids if they had seen Braun; each one responded with a relieved "no." Braun tended to abuse the maids when he was not able to interact with Brianna. One maid in particular was with child, bursting into tears when the Laird spoke to her. She was relieved Braun had not been in residence but fearful that she would be removed from the keep due to her condition. She had no home or family.

As the Laird attempted to console the young maid, he called for the Lady of the Keep. She would be able to help the maid and sort out what must be done. He did not know of the atrocities Braun committed within his own home. He knew Braun to be spoiled and at times needing a swift hand to correct him, but this matter with Brianna must have driven him to lunacy. "I will right these wrongs," Laird Asheboro told the maids and left in search of his wife. "My dove, our son has committed the most horrendous crimes against our maids. Please help them and assure they are taken care of." Lady Asheboro's concern grew as her husband stormed away. Lady Asheboro heard her husband yell for all to hear, "He will never be Laird of Clan Asheboro. We must alert the clan that Braun is no longer welcome in our keep or lands, including Haven Village." Lady Asheboro was in shock to learn what her son had done. She immediately went to seek the maids and did as her husband asked. She loved her son dearly, and it broke her heart that he had become such a vicious man. What happened to the sweet little boy who once brought her flowers and snuggled in her lap? Braun returned from France a changed man.

At thirteen, Braun was sent to stay with the Duke of Laurent. He was to learn about the French court, solidify allied ties, and procure skills from the best military leaders. It was difficult for Braun to readjust to Scottish life after he had spent seven years with the Duke. He was manipulative, sly, and cruel at times. His mother had hoped his demeanor would soften, but it never did.

Braun had spent the last two evenings searching for the Kelpie Ring and still had not found it. How was it possible that his group stumbled upon the Ring and now he could not locate it after retracing his steps? This was the last day of the festival. He would surely be missed at this point. Perhaps his father would send a party out for him and apologize.

On the third morning, Braun found the Kelpie Ring, but he did not know how to reach the water sprite. He thought perhaps that jumping into the pool once again would attract her attention. It had not been a week since their last encounter; she may not be ready to hear of what has transpired. Braun set up his camp near the cool waters. Slowly, a mist began to form, and soon he could not see more than two steps in front of him. As the mist continued to envelop him, Braun began to see a path emerge, leading to a trail deeper into the woods. He was curious but cautious and slowly began to take a few steps on the developing trail. He did not know where he was being led to or how far he was from his campsite.

He came upon a clearing with an ancient tree in the center. Ivy strangled it from all directions and its gnarled roots looked as if they were crawling toward their next victim. In the trunk of the tree was a hollowed out section with a beautiful, gilded mirror placed inside. How odd, Braun thought, for a mirror to be in such a location. He stepped closer to the tree to examine its contents. As he drew closer, he could see people moving within the mirror. *How can this be? Their souls must be trapped by some enchantment.* He watched the mirror with awe and began to realize that the people he was watching were not trapped souls but guests from the festival and games at Asheboro Keep.

The images of the contestants disappeared, and new ones emerged. This time it was within the keep. He saw his father walking toward his chambers and finding an empty room. *All is fine. No one will ever know of my transgressions or of the maids,* Braun thought to himself. As the thoughts ran through his mind, there was the scullery maid he had beaten in anger; then another maid arrived to assist the crying girl who was with his child, though he would deny until his last breath that he had anything to do with the maids. They were speaking to his father, whose mood darkened the more he heard.

"If only I could hear what they were discussing." Braun became slightly uneasy with the images. The mirror faded to black once more. A new image emerged. This time he could hear the conversation as if he were in the room with them. It was his father and mother. They were angry. They had discovered his secrets. The last words he heard his father say were, "He is no son of mine, alert the clan, Braun of Asheboro is no longer my heir. He is not to be permitted on these lands nor Haven Village." The mirror now only showed his reflection. There were no more images dancing or cheering within its gilded confines. Braun's blood boiled with malice. "How dare he strip me of my birthright! This will not stand. He cannot believe them over blood. He is a soft Chieftain. He will see how things will change when I return."

"Hello, curious traveler, have you arrived early to tell me of your keep?" Braun heard the familiar melodious voice of the water sprite and turned to see her standing in the mist. The same flowing silvery hair and venomous green eyes. She was the most beautiful being he had ever seen. The mist allowed him small peeks of her delicate skin, which drove him wild. "My lady, I have come to you as a lowly laird who has been thrown out of his keep and denied his birthright."

The sprite looked intrigued. "Explain, curious traveler. The last we spoke, you were to wed a young maid and become the clan Laird. Have things changed so much in just three days?"

"The maid rejected me once again, embarrassed me in public, and then another laird had the audacity to propose to her. I was enraged and left the keep in search of you. Then the mirror in the tree divulged that my past was revealed to my family." The sprite looked at the tree Braun motioned to, but there was nothing there. The tree was gone, the mirror he spoke of, everything had disappeared.

"My dear traveler, perhaps you are in need of nourishment. I do not see anything other than the mist that surrounds us. Braun looked wild eyed as he searched the clearing for the tree and mirror. "It was here, I swear it on my father's life."

"Do not be distraught, we will seek this tree and mirror." They walked along together in vain. There was no tree or mirror to be found anywhere. Braun sat on the ground, exhausted and humiliated once again. The sprite touched him gently and tried to sooth his emotions. "Do you believe me, fairest sprite?"

"I do, traveler. There is a legend of a mystical forest nymph that wanders the land in search of driving men crazy who dare to seek her out. Perhaps you happened upon her without knowing, and she thought you were leering at her form. As punishment, she may have created the tree and mirror. The images were perhaps meaningless. A simple distraction to allow her to escape."

"Perhaps you are right."

"Now let us see what we can do about your family." Braun sat with the sprite and told her about the keep, his father and mother, and that he was the eldest of six siblings. Two boys and four girls. The next heir would be his younger brother, who was only two years old. What a travesty to think they would surpass him for his younger brother who still wet himself. "Three of my sisters have been betrothed, and the youngest is still not of age to wed. The village is prosperous; with the help of Haven Village we are the wealthiest clan in the highlands."

"Interesting, tell me more about this Haven Village."

Braun continued explaining how the group arrived in Asheboro over seven years before. "They were like nomads wandering the Scottish Highlands. They only carried small parcels and baskets. Some families brought tools of their trade and others foreign fabrics. In the beginning, they kept to themselves and spoke to no one. Then Jada, the head of the community, introduced herself and her family to my father."

"What an interesting name," the sprite interrupted.

"Yes, their clan is very different to ours. My father welcomed them into our lands and provided a small area for them to begin to rebuild their lives. They did not speak of their time before their arrival, stating simply that they could no longer live in their former home."

"I see," the sprite nodded for Braun to continue.

"Then, two years ago, the patriarch of the family appeared. He was disheveled and looked as if someone had held him as a prisoner."

"Please tell me his name?"

"He introduced himself as Maximus." At the mention of Maximus' name, the sprite changed from the ethereal silver glow to a ravenous red but quickly settled herself.

"Is something the matter?" Braun asked.

"No. not at all; I once knew a man by this name. He stole something that was precious to me, and I have not been able to recover it. But we will not speak of this. Continue with your story, my dear Braun." As Braun continued to divulge everything he knew about Haven Village and the Ailey family, Stygian could not contain himself. He had finally found the lost villagers of Luminia.

"This village seems magical," the sprite told Braun.

"It seems so," he concurred. "Now I have nothing. What do I do, dear water sprite?"

"Call me Styx," the sprite replied. "You have become dear to me, Braun. let us not be so formal."

"Thank you, my dear Styx."

"Now, what shall we do about your situation? I did promise you I would help in winning this maiden's heart, but perhaps you would rather seek vengeance. We can tempt her to come to the Ring, and she may meet with me. How about this competing laird, is he as curious as you? Would he enjoy a hunt in these woods? I know exactly what we can do." The sprite's thoughts were coming in such quick succession, Braun could not keep up with each new idea. Finally, she paused for a moment and proceeded to explain. "Return to your keep with these gifts for the happy couple to celebrate their upcoming nuptials."

"But if the images I saw before were true, I will not be allowed into the keep."

"As we are not sure of the source of these images, let us place an enchantment on you. We can disguise you as one of the other clans' men so that you may enter." The sprite produced a small mushroom for Braun to eat.

"Think of what you would like to change about yourself in your mind's eye. Make sure to not exaggerate the features, as the transformation can become painful. Once you consume the mushroom, you will have seven days before the effects will begin to reverse themselves. As for the gifts, you will present them to the couple. The first is pomegranate wine, which the bride should be familiar with; the gift will be the vessel it is contained in. I have enchanted the wine with a sleeping spell. Once she drinks it, she will fall into a gentle slumber. The spell will reverse after two days. No harm will come to her. This will provide you with the opportunity to rescue your damsel from the keep and bring her here for safety. The second gift is for the Laird. It is a quiver and bow."

Braun looked perplexed at such an elaborately decorated gift. "The bow is enchanted. When the Laird uses the bow to hunt, he will be true to his mark. As he makes the fatal blow to the animal the spell will be released from the arrow he pulls from the quiver. As the animal dies from its wound, the Laird will begin to fade as well. He will be stunned into a deep sleep. Many who fall under this spell seem as if dead to the world. The only way to reverse the sleeping spell is if he is kissed by his one true love."

Braun was astonished at the generous gifts he was given. "As you begin this new journey, Braun, remember that timing is everything. You will only have two days to bring

Brianna here and seven days before your spell reverses. As for Cameron, he will be buried alive with no one knowing."

"They will rue the day they dismissed me, " Braun said. "I will take over the keep and be laird. Brianna will eventually understand that I am the better choice and be a dutiful wife. To assure her obedience, I must find a way to imprison her family."

"My, what grand plans you have, Braun of Asheboro.'"

"Thank you, my Lady Styx. How will you know it is me when I return with Brianna?"

"Even though you will be seen differently by the mortals, any magical being will see through the ruse. Only with a mirror will your true reflection be seen by man. Now go and return with your future bride. Remember you have seven days from when you consume your mushroom and two days for her sleeping draft to reverse.

CHAPTER 8

A Vision and a Plan

THE VERNAL EQUINOX celebration was more than a success; it was a true festival of peace and unions. The clans reveled in their triumphs, and many maidens were betrothed to strengthen clan alliances. The gem of all the events was the announcement of Laird Cedar-Kellen to wed Lady Brianna Ailey of Haven Village. The only shadow throughout the event was the disappearance of Braun. No one could locate him. Even though he was no longer welcomed in the Asheboro lands, his father wanted to assure his son knew the gravity of his situation and would hopefully become the respectful man he once knew, in which case he would consider lifting his ban.

Brianna and Cameron were in heaven. Cameron asked Laird Asheboro if he could stay on for a sennight to allow him time to meet with Brianna's family and begin their wedding plans. The Laird joyfully extended Cameron's stay in the keep. "It would be an honor to hold your wedding in Asheboro, if you so wish," Laird Asheboro stated.

"Thank you, Laird Asheboro, for your kindness and generosity. I would like to hold the ceremony at my stronghold, Cawdor Castle."

"I understand. She has won your heart and those of your people. How better to celebrate than holding your ceremony at your keep. I have traveled beyond our lands for tournaments but have never had the honor of visiting Cawdor. It must be a wonder."

"Aye, it is. The gardens are the most coveted in our clan. You must come and stay for a visit with us."

"I would be most honored. I will await your invitation." Cameron had one last situation he wanted to address: the matter of Braun and Brianna.

"Laird Asheboro, even though we will not be family by blood, I consider you as a dear uncle. I would like to speak with Braun and hope we can reconcile our broken ties. I understand his heartbreak. I hope he will one day find a maiden to love again." Laird Asheboro thanked Cameron for his generous nature. He then revealed that Braun had disappeared the day of the opening games after his assault on Brianna.

"I see. Perhaps I can locate him. He is most likely licking his wounds from embarrassment. May I have permission for Braun to enter your lands for us to mend our ties? I do not want my future bride to be in fear of his retaliation once we are wed. Her family is everything to her and she will not leave them if they are in any danger."

Laird Asheboro was silent for a few moments pondering Cameron's request. "I will grant this request, but only under the condition that it is you who escorts him and no other."

"Agreed." Cameron extended his arm for the Lairds to shake on this pact.

The Ailey Home

Brianna was over the moon. She could not believe that her dreams would soon be a reality. The man who tantalized her nightly dreamscape escapades would soon be her husband. As Jada and the rest of the family prepared their home for a new guest, the air was filled with excitement. Celeste and Aurora came to help prepare a feast for Laird Cedar-Kellen. Brianna's brothers came to assist their father to assure all the household items needing fixing were completed. As Brianna sat with her mother and sisters, they began to put together Brianna's hope chest.

A beautiful oak chest was made by her father, carved with the likeness of thistles. He placed a special enchantment on the vessel to allow its contents to never be harmed. They first placed the cherished wrap Jada had made for her when they were escaping Solasta, followed by the small box of earth Maximus had also gifted her upon their escape. Then came the delicate dresses and under garments. As she had for her two older daughters, Jada created a beautiful quilt for Brianna to place on her marriage bed. Each small stitch was placed with care. The quilt was decorated with multitudes of roses intermingled with tulips and lilies. In the center was a scene of their entire family lounging among the tranquil waters of the Solastian pool. It radiated harmony and peace, and Brianna knew she would never be alone. Soon, Laird Cedar-Kellen would arrive to meet the entire family and begin the wedding preparations. Brianna wanted to have a small handfasting ceremony in Asheboro and then a grand wedding celebration at Cawdor Castle. As part of her dowry, Maximus fashioned two ornate wedding rings for the couple to wear. Rather than a simple golden band for each, he placed an ancient fae blessing within the design written in the fae language.

"Two souls apart become as one as they wear these rings of gold. May the Elders bless this union from now and beyond, guiding them through weather fair and stormy."

To any mortal, they would seem as elaborate Celtic drawings with filigree. Maximus presented the bands to Brianna and said, "Any future Laird and Lady must have matching sets of rings to display their bond as one." Tears began to flow from her eyes as she knew how much her father sacrificed for her and their family. As their hands touched in the exchange of the small box holding the couple's wedding bands, Maximus stiffened, and his hands began to clutch Brianna's in a painful grip.

Jada ran to him and placed her hands on his chest. Maximus needed to focus on the vision at hand. Tears began to stream down his face. Brianna knew this vision was about her, and if they did not change the course of the events as they did so many years ago there may not be a wedding or a Haven Village. "Mother, what is he seeing? Is it Braun? Is Stygian coming? Mother please tell me." As the Ailey siblings circled their parents, Jada began to speak slowly.

"Braun never disappeared; he has found the Kelpie Ring. Stygian is disguised as a water sprite. He is still in Solasta, but the enchantment has been weakened. Braun plans to take Brianna as his bride and kill Laird Cedar-Kellen."

"No," Brianna screamed.

"This cannot be. How will all this transpire?" asked Celeste.

Maximus was using all his strength to continue the vision, but was quickly weakening. "Stygian gave Braun an elixir with a bow and quiver. Braun is coming for you." The last words Jada spoke in a solemn tone. As the vision was beginning to fade away, Laird Cedar-Kellen entered the Ailey home with gifts for all.

He immediately dropped everything, thinking that Maximus was deathly ill and wanted to assist the family. River and Rune broke from the circle and went to Cameron. The Laird was deeply concerned. "He is having a fit. We must assist him."

"He is not having a fit," River assured the Laird. "We will explain all in due course. It is almost over." Wanting to trust his new relations, Cameron steadied himself and sat.

River and Rune returned to the family circle. Finally, Maximus was released from the vision, and he collapsed into Jada's arms. "They are in danger, my love. We must tell the Lairds of Asheboro and Cedar-Kellen," Maximus said in a hushed tone. Fear in her eyes, Jada knew it must have been serious if Maximus wanted to divulge their story to the Lairds.

"I will tell you more my love, but first I must rest." River gently helped his father up. Maximus, realizing Laird Cedar-Kellen witnessed his vision, apologized for his current state. "I am sorry, Laird Cedar-Kellen, that I will not be able to entertain this evening. Do not worry, for I will be well. Jada and the rest of my family will have plenty of stories to regale you with." The Laird nodded in understanding and wished Maximus well. Jada looked at Maximus, and he replied, "It is well my dear. He will receive the message well. He is part of our family now and must know what is to come."

Jada turned to the Laird and smiled warmly. "Thank you so much for the beautiful gifts, Laird Cedar-Kellen." Cameron, still in shock, nodded and assisted in retrieving the items he dropped. "Please, call me Cameron, if we are to be family no need to stand on ceremony."

"As you wish my Laird, I mean Cameron." Jada began to laugh as they fumbled with the packages the Laird brought.

For each of Brianna's sisters, he provided honey from his hives with small toys for their children. For the brothers he brought a new hip flask for their hunts. As for Maximus and Jada, Cameron presented his family tartan for them to wear. The colors were rich blues, yellows, and purples. This was a true honor, as tartans were only meant for the family of the clan members. He did not forget his future bride.

He presented her with an exquisite pearl necklace to match the tartan and brooch she had received prior to their betrothal. "What are they?" Brianna asked. "I have never seen such wondrous stones." Cameron explained that they were pearls from the sea.

"They are created when something irritates an oyster. As a defense, it begins to coat the irritant with aragonite and conchiolin. It is a natural gemstone from the sea."

"I have never been to the sea, my Laird. These are truly a treasure." Brianna had never been presented with such lavish gifts.

"These pearls do not compare to your radiance, my love," Cameron said.

The exchange between the couple was more than love—it was fate. Anyone who looked at them would instantly know they were one mind, body, and soul. "As your father is not well, I will return tomorrow in hopes of planning our wedding festival." Brianna reached out to Cameron and begged him to stay, for there was much to discuss.

The family guided Cameron to their sitting room. Cameron felt as if he was a lamb being led for the slaughter, but he eased his nerves. As everyone sat around the room, Jada began to speak.

"My Laird, once again, we thank you for your generosity and gifts. Our family has been blessed by the fates that our Brianna was placed in your path. We must begin to explain our past to assure that our future remains. Our story is dark, but we hope it will end in the light. First, do you know anything about the Fae people?"

Cameron laughed and said, "No such people exist. My nursemaid would tell me stories of fae traveling between our worlds with mystical powers, and how a war broke out one day. Mortals were no longer allowed to travel between the realms and the fae have disappeared since. When she spoke of the fae, they were always kind beings with foreign items to sell. She never spoke ill words of the fae people."

"Your nurse maid was a wise woman," interjected Jada.

"You cannot believe her stories," Cameron replied.

"What if we told you that the fae have always existed among humans?"

Cameron sat quietly while attempting to understand what Jada was explaining to him. "Are you telling me that the stories my nursemaid told were fact?"

"Yes, my dear Laird. She may have even been a fae herself. Did you ever notice her hiding her ears? Or perhaps she could touch you and you felt calm and warm?"

Cameron thought for a moment. "Yes, all those things."

"Then she was a fae. Many fae would leave the realm of Solasta to live among the humans. Solasta was rich in all things, but the rising of a Fae King, Stygian, began to change how the realm interacted with nature and his philosophies became dark. The once-vibrant and prosperous world of Solasta began to deteriorate, and our people had to flee into the mortal world."

"So, you expect me to believe I was raised by a fairy all my childhood and that fae live among us?"

"Yes," Jada replied calmly. "We are a peaceful people and stay out of the matters of mortal affairs."

"We?" Cameron retorted. "Are you fae?" Each family member at that moment revealed their subtle disguises. River, Rune, and Ronan, who wore their hair long and down, pulled their hair back into ponytails. Jada, Celeste, and Aurora removed their head scarves. Brianna pulled her hair back to reveal the same pointed ears. Cameron was in shock, not realizing he had been holding his breath the entire time, and he began to gasp for air.

He knew he was safe and no harm would come to him, but he still did not know what to think. "Is this why you were able to heal me and not leave a scar?" Brianna answered with a whisper.

"Yes… my power is the ability to heal others even on the brink of death."

"This is why you are the village healer."

"Yes," Brianna stated confidently. "I use poultices and salves as any other healer does but there are times that more is needed. In those moments I use my power to heal. If a person is past the brink, I can ease their pain and allow them a gentle transition into the other world."

Cameron was in awe. He could not speak for a full five minutes as he sat with the deluge of information that was just revealed to him. Brianna slowly stepped forward and placed her gift on his lap, thinking he now no longer wanted to marry her. Stunned by her actions, he looked at her and said, "You think me so feeble minded that I would now reject you for your gifts and talents?"

"No, my Laird. I would never think such a thing, but I do know many mortals would not want to associate with the fae. There are numerous stories of our dark fae that permeate the mortal world. Fear usually strikes them and they do more harm than good." Cameron stood slowly and laid a gentle kiss on Brianna's forehead.

"May I?" he asked, as he raised the pearl necklace. She nodded with approval and he placed the necklace over her head and onto her delicate neck. She looked up to Cameron and smiled with embarrassment that she would think he would ever waver in his love for her.

"Thank you Laird Cedar-Kellen."

"Cameron," he said.

"Thank you, Cameron."

"We are most pleased that you have taken our news so well. Now for the not so good news."

"There's more?" Cameron exclaimed.

"Yes, and it involves you and Brianna. Braun was furious after your last encounter. It seems that he was able to find the Kelpie Ring from which we escaped. Maximus was able to seal it, keeping Stygian in Solasta and the mortal realm safe. Unfortunately, when Maximus made his return to the mortal realm, it weakened the enchantments we placed to seal it. We are safe for now, but we do not know for how much longer."

Jada continued to describe the parts of the vision she was able to see. Cameron began to pace the room as he heard the news. "Braun is planning some sort of attack or coup. We do not know the details of this, or how it will happen, until we meet with Maximus. Only he can tell us the entire vision."

"Did you see anything that could help me prepare for Braun's attack?"

"We must be careful, Laird Cameron. Even though we can alter the future, there is more at stake. It is not simply stopping Braun. It is stopping the Dark Fae King from entering the mortal realm. If he were ever to gain access to this world, we all will be doomed. The one thing I can say without a doubt is that Braun is within these woods and near Haven Village.

We must somehow alert Laird Asheboro without telling him about Solasta. He may not be as understanding as you are. He gave us shelter and in exchange we became a prosperous village for him, but he is not comfortable with magic or the fae. We will only reveal ourselves if there is no other way to save the clan."

"I understand," Cameron said.

"Cameron, make sure you do not seek Braun. We do not know when he will strike. Brianna will be safe here with us. She will not venture anywhere outside of Haven Village without an escort."

"Thank you for trusting me with your secret. No one will ever know of the fae, not even my brother, Robert." After such an eye-opening first family meeting, The Aileys and Cameron attempted to enjoy a family meal. Jada took a plate to her recovering husband to assure he would regain his strength and help the family create a plan to provide safety for Brianna, her future groom, and all of Asheboro.

CHAPTER 9

The Lost Son Returns

BRAUN MADE HIS way from the Kelpie Ring to the outer lands of Clan Asheboro. He hoped what he had witnessed in the magic mirror was false, a mere joke played on him by the forest nymph. Before stepping foot into his clan land, he steadied himself, taking a moment to think of his current plan. "What has driven me to this? Is Brianna worth the consequences of such a plan?" Braun continued to question himself as he held tight in one hand to the mushroom that would transform him and the elixir that would provide him with the woman of his dreams in the other. He felt as if he was being driven by madness.

Perhaps he should allow his father an opportunity to right the injustices meted against him. But then he remembered how he was embarrassed in front of the crowds, being dismissed as if he were a small child. His blood began to boil once again with the anger he felt. *One more chance, Father, before I take what is rightfully mine,* Braun said to himself. He walked into his land confidently. He passed through Haven

Village first to pay the Ailey family a visit. As he began to knock on their door, Braun felt a presence behind him followed by two large shadows. He slowly turned to see who would dare approach him unannounced.

To his amazement, it was Rune and Ronan, Brianna's older brothers. He smiled a sly grin and extended his hand to greet them. The Ailey brothers did not return the greeting. "What are you doing here, Braun?" spoke Ronan. "You have been banned from these lands and are no longer welcome. Brianna is betrothed to Laird Cedar-Kellen. We will be celebrating their handfasting in ten days after the King's arrival before they leave for Cawdor Castle to meet his clansmen." Braun attempted to remain cool as the words Ronan spoke pierced his soul adding fuel to the fire burning within him.

"Oh, I see," he replied. "Then I will make my way to the keep to gather my belongings before I leave."

The brothers did not like Braun's behavior. They knew something was afoot, for normally Braun would have exploded with the news of Brianna's betrothal and his exile from the lands. Braun excused himself and left. Rune looked to his brother. "There is something wrong, but I cannot place my finger on it. Braun has changed, and not for the better." The Ailey brothers watched Braun as he walked away, muttering to himself.

Braun was now resolute that he would take Brianna for his own. His thoughts began to grow darker the closer he moved toward Asheboro Keep. Perhaps the water Sprite,

Lady Styx, would be able to grant him lands within her realm, or better yet he would rid himself of his father and take the Lairdship for himself. No one would be able to stop him, especially his two-year-old brother."

Continuing on his walk to the keep, Braun noticed the villagers turning their backs on him. No one greeted him. The men in the village entered their homes without a second glance. The visions in the mirror were true; he was no longer welcome in Clan Asheboro. Only his father could fix this. As he made his way to the entrance of the keep, two burly clans men, Angus and Callum, blocked his way. "We are sorry, Braun, but we are under strict orders to not allow you into the keep or on our lands."

"Angus, this is truly madness, a simple misunderstanding. Please allow me to pass. I would like to speak with my father."

Angus and Callum looked at each other. They were not friends of Braun's and disliked his treatment of the women within the keep. Callum decided he would talk with the Laird to see if Braun could be granted a meeting. "Angus, will you be all right if I were to leave?"

"Of course, Callum, do you think me a wee bairn just born and weak?"

Angus was twice the size of Braun and could best anyone in a wrestling match. Braun knew if he were to make any move he would be done for.

Braun was handsome and muscular, but he was not 6'6" and made of iron. Angus could crush him if he wanted. As Callum walked away, a thought came to Braun. Why not put him to sleep with the elixir? Brianna did not need to drink it all, did she? He would place a few drops of the elixir in his hip flask and share a drink with the giant.

Once asleep, he could walk his way into the keep and speak with his father. "Would you like a drink, Angus? It must be tiring standing here day and night with no rest. While I was away, I encountered a caravan of nomads. They gave me some of the most delicious wine I have ever tasted. Would you like to try it?" Angus, always loving a good drink, could not turn down the offer. Braun set his pouch on the ground to rummage for the elixir and his hip flask. He quickly placed four drops of the elixir in the flask. He pretended to take a taste before handing it to Angus.

Braun hoped the effects would take place quickly so no one would be able to see what had transpired. At the very moment Braun handed Angus his hip flask, Callum walked out. "Unfortunately Braun, your father is currently indisposed. He is making the preparations for the arrival of King Arthur and his new bride, Guinevere. He did mention if you truly would like to meet with him and speak of your transgressions, he would meet you in a sennight. At that time, our humble King Arthur will be present and all matters situated for his highness. The sovereign and his bride are touring the realm as a newly wed couple. We have been blessed to be chosen as his first resting location before continuing his journey to the Isle of Skye and beyond. We will have festivities and banquets for all to enjoy."

Braun thought this would be perfect. He would wait until the arrival of the King, then spring his trap. *Everyone will be distracted by the arrival of the King along with the festivities. I will be able to kidnap Brianna, give Cameron his special gift, and escape without notice.*

Realizing he had given the flask to Angus he quickly retrieved it, spilling its contents on the ground. "Forgive me, Angus, I was so moved by my father's good fortune that I could not contain myself. I hope to be in his good graces once again and perhaps be able to meet our King and his bride." Angus and Callum looked at each other with apprehension. They did not like the manner in which Braun was acting and hoped to speak with the Laird to discuss this arrangement. Braun gathered his things and made his way back into the forest.

Walking back to the Kelpie Ring, he was elated to tell Lady Styx of the new information he had acquired. The once-uncomfortable and at times frightening forest became Braun's domain. He was sure-footed without a care in the world. He finally arrived at the Ring and began to unpack his things. The now-familiar mist began to envelop him again. His Lady Styx would be arriving soon. As the mist engulfed Braun, he began to feel drowsy. This was odd, as it had never happened before. Slowly Braun laid himself down on the pallet he made, drifting off to sleep.

Stygian began to search Braun's memories to see what new information he could find. He saw the interaction with the village and clansmen. What a fool for him to use his elixir on the guards. He then probed further to listen to the guards' conversation. *Arthur is coming! That will mean Merlin will be with him*, thought Stygian. It had been many years since he had seen his rival. Merlin should have been the Fae King, but Stygian had other plans and had swayed the Elders to select him instead.

If it were not for Stygian being willing to reveal the Elders' clandestine secrets through blackmail, he would have been dismissed. Of course, Merlin would never resort to such tactics. Only Maximus was as powerful as Merlin. This knowledge is what led to Merlin's sacrifice. He knew that one of them must stay behind if Solasta were to have a chance of ever surviving. Merlin graciously left the Elders' council and proceeded to leave the fae world. He would make his way through the mortal realm and hone his skills.

Stygian continued his probe into Braun's mind. He became enraged that Braun had not proceeded with their original plan. Waiting a sennight would make it more difficult for Stygian to gain the necessary power to break the enchantment of the Kelpie Ring. Furthermore, if Merlin and Maximus were to discover his plan, they would surely thwart him. Stygian's physical being was locked in the fae realm, but he was able to penetrate the Ring with his powers of mind control. As he continued to use the powers from the crystals he'd collected, it took longer for them to regenerate. He could not continue the charade of impersonating a water sprite for much longer.

This game would not last forever. He must act now. As Braun was in a deep sleep, using his powers of projection, Stygian began to manipulate the elements. He wrapped the young man's body with vines and grass, creating a living cocoon. This would protect Braun from the elements and assure he stays alive long enough for Stygian to complete his plan. After Braun was secured, Stygian needed to rest and allow the crystals to regenerate. "Now. How to get into the keep?"

Stygian pondered the many ways he would destroy Haven Village and Asheboro Keep. Having spent so much time with Braun, he knew he would be very capable of impersonating the young man. Using the mud and clay from the Kelpie Ring, Stygian created a golem of Braun that he would be able to manipulate to his will. The creature would be tethered to Braun's body. No one would know the difference between the original and the replica. The only difference would be the impersonator would require constant water to survive.

If he were in an altercation, he would simply return to his original state of mud and clay, severing the connection between himself and the true Braun. The assault to this being would reveal he was not mortal but an enchantment, leaving Braun vulnerable, or even dead. *Another day of rest*, thought Stygian. *Then I can set my trap.*

Stygian slept well with the joy that he would soon be creating chaos and destruction to the mortal realm while procuring the magical talents of the Ailey family. If he was lucky, he could perhaps also acquire Merlin's powers. Then no one would be able to stop him.

There was one day left before the arrival of Arthur and his new bride. The keep was abuzz with maids cleaning and preparing rooms for the visitors. Laird Asheboro met with Maximus to make arrangements for entertainment and gifts to present to the King. Maximus was honored to be held in such high esteem within the Asheboro Clan. He assured the Laird all would be well and that Haven Village would have plenty of spectacles to entertain the King and his entourage.

As the men spoke of the plans and arrangements, Maximus asked the Laird if he had seen his son since the incident at the fete. "Aye," said the Laird. "Braun came to the keep almost a week ago. He was stopped by Callum and Angus. As I had just discovered Arthurs' coming to the keep with his new bride, I did not have the patience or foresight to want to speak with him. I asked Callum to send a message to Braun asking him to come again after the arrival of Arthur."

"Was that wise?" Maximus inquired.

Laird Asheboro was uncertain if Braun would create chaos while the King was in residence. "If my son has the misguided thought of creating mayhem within our lands, it would definitely be on his head and not the clan's. I hope Braun is able to control himself, even though he has not been able to show me his restraint as of yet. The King in residence should steer him into a more neutral mindset. Above all else, Braun wants to be seen as a charismatic equal and not as an abusive madman."

"I see," Maximus replied in a thoughtful manner. "Perhaps we should include a few sentries to keep an eye out for him in the event he decides not to be rational. We will have Cameron bring a few extra men from his keep to Asheboro until the King has left."

Laird Asheboro nodded in agreement then asked Maximus, "When Braun comes to see me, would you be willing to be part of the counsel?"

"Of course, my Laird. It would be an honor."

"Thank you, Maximus. Since your arrival, you have become a great confidant and friend. I cannot condone what my son has done. I thought I was a good father, but it seems that I have failed him in some way."

"Do not place the burden or blame on yourself, my lord. You provided all that Braun needed to become your successor. He was the one who chose this path for himself. Whether it was due to the company he kept or his own inflated ego, he chose to be dishonorable and abusive."

"You are right, Maximus, but it is still hard to grapple with. We did provide all he ever wanted and perhaps our fault lay in spoiling him as a child and not providing the proper boundaries every young child needs in their formative years. Perhaps I should not have sent him to France."

"Do not dwell on this, Laird Asheboro."

The men continued to speak of the upcoming visit and began to dispatch messages to the surrounding clans to assure all protocols were followed. Maximus spoke with Cameron and asked for him to extend his stay in Asheboro to provide a unified front if and when Braun were to arrive.

Arthurs' Arrival

The keep could hear the caravan of travelers and heralding trumpets announcing the King was near. Laird Asheborohad runners posted every few miles to estimate when the King would arrive. It was a spectacle watching the royal guard march in unison with the elaborate carriages following behind. Banners swayed with the wind, showcasing the royal family's crest. The sun shone, birds sang, the sky a gorgeous blue, all heralding the arrival of the King. No one could have wished for a more perfect day. Nothing could possibly ruin this day.

At the keep, the Asheboro and Ailey families waited with bated breath. They hoped Braun would not arrive until the next day. The Laird did not want to handle family affairs in front of the King. Haven Village was decorated with luxurious fabrics and ribbons providing a magical look. The houses were white washed and spruced up with new thatch. The villagers donned their best attire to greet the King. Arthur and Guinevere began to see the village as they crested the hill toward Asheboro keep. The fates were definitely in favor of this land and people. The rich colors of the ribbons and fabrics were otherworldly, seeming to dance with the wind in a beautiful ballet orchestrated by mother nature.

As the carriages approached Haven Village, it was as its name described, a safe space for all. The village was not of this world. The air was fresher, the crops more bountiful, the livestock hardy. They truly were a blessed clan. The carriage stopped for a moment as four beautiful maidens approached the guard and presented them with food and water. The knights were not always accustomed to such luxuries and glanced at each other. "We mean no harm but to welcome you to Haven Village. We have pomegranate wine for the King and his Queen with pastries for them to enjoy if they would like to partake of a small meal before continuing on their journey."

Arthur overheard the ladies speaking and peered outside his carriage window. "Please come forward, young maidens. What are your names?"

"Emma, Madeline, Lilyana, and Emily," Responded the girls, bowing low.

"What beautiful names for such lovely and generous maidens. Please forgive my knights and their skepticism. Rarely do they find themselves welcomed. I will soon have these perceptions changed in time. Please tell me of your offerings."

The maidens smiled and approached the carriage. The rest of the village began to come out to witness the exchange. "We have prepared baskets filled with breads, cheeses, and water for the knights to enjoy on their way to the keep. And for you, your highness, a gift basket for you and your beautiful bride." Lilyana presented the stunning basket made of wicker, decorated with lavender and other herbs. Inside the basket was a bottle of their most prized pomegranate wine, a loaf of bread, pastries filled with jams, and an elaborate cloth for Guinevere to use to make a dress.

"These gifts are too generous," Arthur stated.

"Nothing is too much for our King. Our lands are prosperous and we are simply the stewards of it."

"How wise for such young people. You have been taught well. Thank you for your generosity. Perhaps we shall see you at the keep during our stay."

"Tonight there's a feast in your honor and the entire village will be present; we shall see you, Your Highnesses." The group finished their exchange and the entourage began once again to travel to the keep. The villagers were in awe of the King and his kind demeanor. Once the carriage cleared the village, the last runner was dispatched to the keep.

Laird Asheboro and Maximus were on pins and needles as they awaited the arrival of the King. They saw the final runner making his way to the keep and began to have all the servants move into position in the front for inspection. The absence of Braun was felt, making the families uneasy, but they steadied themselves just in time for the first knight to arrive at the entrance of Asheboro keep. The knights filed in and created a circle for the King's carriage to enter. The carriage arrived with its occupants ready to disembark after such a long journey.

Arthur was the first to emerge from the carriage. He was older but virile, handsome, and muscular. To the surprise of all, the King was dressed in a simple tunic and leggings. The only item denoting he was a king was his crown. All knelt in his presence awaiting for him to acknowledge them. "Thank you all for the grand welcome. Please rise. I would like to introduce you to my wife and Queen of Camelot, Guinevere." A roar of applause erupted from the crowd as the flawless Guinevere emerged from the carriage. Her hair was golden brown with flecks of blonde placed in an elaborate plait adorned with flowers and hanging to her waist. Unlike her husband, she was dressed in a gown fit for a queen made of velvet and long bell sleeves. It was intricately designed with filigree throughout. She gave a shy smile to the crowd and allowed her husband to continue with the introductions.

All was going well, and both Maximus and Laird Asheboro were relieved once all the proper introductions were made. The servants were dismissed to their duties, and the villagers began to disperse to their homes when a runaway horse stampeded through the villagers with an unconscious rider. Quickly, the Ailey brothers ran to the scared animal and were able to calm it. They realized the rider was Braun. His skin was cold to the touch and he was barely breathing.

They called for Brianna to assist, but she had already entered the keep with Laird Cedar-Kellen. "Do not despair, Braun, we will help you. Someone please run to the keep and notify the Laird his son is at death's door, send Brianna with her supplies. We should take him to the keep. He cannot lie out here in the elements if he is to have any chance of living." Rune interjected, "Ronan, have you forgotten what he has done? Have you forgotten the edict made by our Laird?" River agreed with Rune. "I have not forgotten his evil deeds, but he is a dying man. No matter a person's past, they deserve a chance to repent and gain forgiveness if it is possible. If he survives, we will be blessed by the fates. His father can then decide what should happen next." River and Rune were still apprehensive about bringing Braun to the keep but decided to be unified with their brother and carry the dying Braun to his former home.

As they began to lift the feeble young man, he whispered, "Water. Please, water." River could not deny a dying man his last wish. He removed his hip flask and slowly allowed Braun to drink from it. As Braun began to drink his color slowly began to return. "Perhaps he will make it after all," said Ronan.

CHAPTER 10

Golem In Our Midst

THE BANQUET HALL was warm and inviting. The King and his Queen sat at the dais with the Asheboro family flanking their right side. The Ailey family was honored in being invited to join them at the head table and sat to the left of the King. Maximus was beginning to feel distressed when he noticed his sons had not entered the keep or hall yet. Jada sensed his apprehension and tried to soothe his nerves.

"All will be well, my love."

"I am not sure, Jada. Something does not seem as it is. Why haven't our boys arrived yet? They knew the importance of today. Braun is still somewhere plotting, and Stygian has a hand in it."

"Have you had another vision?" asked Jada.

"No, my sweet wife, I have not. Remember my visions are subject to change when a person makes a final decision.

As it stands, Braun intends to harm us, take Brianna, and rule the clan. We cannot allow this to happen; we must change his course somehow."

Maximus was becoming frantic. Jada excused herself and her husband for a moment to allow Maximus to use his powers to search for his sons. Brianna saw her parents leave the dais and looked for reassurance from her mother but none was to come. Her brothers were missing and her parents were leaving the banquet hall. Worrisome thoughts began to flood her mind. *What was happening? Were they in danger?* At the same moment her parents were about to step outside, her brothers burst into the hall carrying Braun in a pitiful state.

The hall gasped with surprise to see the once-future Laird within the walls of the keep on the brink of death. Ronan spoke first. "He has not spoken since we left the village. He simply asked for water and became unconscious. Please forgive our rude entrance, Your Highness. We did not want the death of the son of our Laird on our hands. We do not know what transpired or how he came to be in this state, but we know our sister, Brianna, can heal him or assist in his journey to transition from this world."

"No forgiveness needed, my young man. Laird Asheboro, go to your son and make any arrangements you may need. I can entertain myself and your guests. I will dispatch a rider to send word to my advisor, Merlin.

If Brianna needs assistance, he will be able to aid her." Laird Asheboro looked at the King in shock for such a generous offer.

"Is he not a seer and mage? Can he be trusted?" Laird Asheboro asked.

"You must be jesting, Rodric."

"I do not, Your Highness."

"Yes, Merlin is my advisor and mage. He can create spells and see the future. He can heal and provide wisdom in the most bleak of situations."

"I see," replied Laird Asheboro. "Then send for him. My son is worth everything to me. We may have had a falling out, but I would never wish him death. Perhaps the world will mature him after this and one day he may earn the right to return to the keep. He must first right his wrongs before I am ever to consider him a son of mine, but I must give him a chance for redemption."

A knight was sent to retrieve Merlin while the King and his entourage continued to enjoy the banquet. The Ailey brothers assisted the servants in bringing Braun into his former bed chamber and settling him for the evening. Braun continued to ask for water while he struggled in and out of consciousness. Most believed those to be the wishes of a dying man. They acquiesced to his requests, continuing to bring the young man water and tea until Brianna was located. They never once thought it odd that he did not ask for more sustenance, simply water.

Once the servants and brothers left, the golem slowly

rose from the bed and began to stretch his body. The continued supply of water allowed for him to recover his strength. Thankful that no one had rummaged through his belongings, the golem began to open his satchel. Among the items were the sleeping elixir and the bow with arrows. Also within the sack was a cloak with a crystal amulet. This was to be used to aid in his escape. He knew there was not much time before someone would return. He wrapped the wedding gifts in a velvet pouch for the future couple and placed them on the bed with a simple note: "Congratulations to Laird Cedar-Kellan and Lady Brianna."

Slowly, Braun emerged from his chambers. Not wanting to be discovered, he stayed within the shadows. The house was alive with movement due to the arrival of the King. He needed to know where the King's bedchambers were located along with those of Brianna and Cameron. As honored guests, they would have the best accommodations. He continued through the keep until he heard a group of chambermaids. They were so excited to be able to meet the King and Queen of England, here from the fabled castle Camelot. One of the maids mentioned they were located in the north tower.

Perfect, Braun thought. "Now to locate Cameron's and Brianna's chambers," he whispered to himself. If the King and Queen were in the north tower, that would place Cameron and Brianna in the west tower. The other towers were for military purposes and family living quarters. Braun decided to return to his chambers and wait for his plan to unfurl. No one noticed he had left his chambers. He laid the gifts on the side table and rested.

Brianna gently walked into Braun's chamber with her basket filled with herbs and poultices. He felt cool to the touch. His skin was pale and muddied. She did not know of his ailment, only that he continuously wanted water. She had a pitcher brought in to make tea. *Perhaps the healing herbs will fortify him and allow the Laird and King to question him,* Brianna thought. As she worked, the golem opened his eyes to watch her every move. She was light as a feather in her touch. Each movement was a dance that called to him. Even though the golem was a creature made of mud, it still held feelings and distorted memories that were tethered to the true Braun lying in the forest. Stygian was able to use the golems' sight to view the happenings within the keep. Seeing the beauty caring for his golem made him want her.

The dress she wore was of a rich purple hue with gold embroidery. The seamstress who created it must have been a master, for the garment fit Brianna like a second skin. All her charms were on display; from slim waist to supple breasts, Brianna was truly exquisite. She would be the most radiant jewel in his crown. Not wanting to interrupt her preparations, the golem continued to enjoy watching her. "It is a shame we did not marry," he said.

"Braun! You have awoken. I did not mean to disturb your recovery."

"You did not disturb my slumber. Your fragrance of roses was what tempted my senses."

Brianna blushed at Braun's' comments. She quickly turned and retrieved the tea she was making for him. "I have heard you want solely water; that is not enough sustenance to help a man of your stature recover. I have made you a restorative. Drink up." Braun gave her a devilish grin and slowly drank the hot tea.

It invigorated him to his core. She then brought over a small plate with fruit, meat, and cheeses for him to consume. "Make sure to eat. Your father and King Arthur will be visiting you soon. The state you arrived in, they want to assure you are safe and the keep is not in any danger, or the kingdom, for that matter. King Arthur has been gracious enough to summon his mage, Merlin, to visit with you as well." At the mention of Merlin's name, Braun dropped the cup of tea and began to tremble. Brianna thought he was suffering from his maladies or that the tea may have triggered a negative reaction. She quickly placed her hands on him to attempt to soothe his body. He tried to stop her but was too slow to react.

Once Brianna's hands touched him, they began to glow, but his body did not feel like that of other mortals. He was cold and clammy. She could not feel the rhythm of his heart in his chest. *What is going on?* she thought. Her eyes became wide. "What have you done?" Braun could no longer wait to execute his plan. Still trembling, he rose from the bed and grabbed Brianna. She attempted to free herself from his grasp, but her struggles were in vain.

She tried to claw at his face and merely left a scratch. The wound did not bleed. "What magic is this?" she asked as his marks quickly disappeared.

"Do not worry lass. Soon you will be with me in my kingdom. Now be an obedient wife and stay silent while I get us out of here."

"I will never be your wife! How dare you touch me. Release me at once."

The imposter tightened his grip, leaving bruises on her delicate skin. She began to scream for help, and he quickly placed his hand over her mouth. Growing more frantic, Brianna attempted to bite his hand to only return with a mouth full of mud. Her eyes widened with terror, not knowing what Braun had turned into.

The golem knew he had to incapacitate Brianna quickly before she created too much noise bringing the keep to her aid. Releasing her mouth for a moment to grab the elixir Brianna had one last attempt to scream for help. Her cry was quickly stifled by the liquid Braun was attempting to pour into her mouth. "Now, now, my sweeting. Take the elixir so that you can be well rested." Brianna fought to the very end, spitting into Braun's face as he attempted to pour more of the elixir into her mouth. She hoped the few drops that she did swallow would not be enough to take effect. She began to feel drowsy. Her efforts were no longer strong enough to stop who she thought to be Braun from finishing what he'd begun.

As her eyes began to close, the golem lifted her, quickly placing her small frame into his trunk. The last thing Brianna remembered seeing was her reflection in the mirror of the wardrobe. The odd thing was the person carrying her was not Braun but a creature made of mud. Mirrors always showed a person's true nature and anyone under an enchantment would not be able to hide their true facade. "How is this possible? Who are you?" Brianna attempted to yell at the creature. Knowing that she would soon succumb to the elixir, Brianna attempted one last spell before she was in total darkness. Hoping her father would be able to decipher her cryptic message, Brianna held onto her amulet tightly to allow it to prick her palm. She slowly sang:

"Blood of my Blood, giver of life, I now journey to the river of death. Blood of my Blood, life after death, may my journey be calm and light. Blood of my blood, the River Styx, the Ring will forever be my peace and sight."

Brianna's hand began to glow. She held tight to her amulet and used the last of her strength to focus her powers on delivering her amulet to her eldest sister, Celeste. The amulet disappeared in a bright light, shocking the golem disguised as Braun; for a moment he was blinded and nearly dropped Brianna. The golem knew there was some sort of magic at work. Stygian had limited powers while using the golem. He needed to work quickly to guide the golems' return to the Kelpie Ring.

He dismissed the magic as Brianna laid limp in his arms. He placed her in the trunk and closed the lid. "Success!"

Stygian could not wait for the golem to return with his prize. Brianna was captured and he had slipped away with no one noticing his movements; he was able to convince a chambermaid to place the bow and arrows into Laird Cedar-Kellen's bed chamber. His plan was in motion. With the small amount of magic he was able to use, Stygian's golem cloaked the trunk he had Brianna in and transported her to the Kelpie Ring. All that was left was for Cameron to hunt with the bow. Once this transpired, the Laird would fall into the deepest sleep as close to death as possible to be buried alive by his clansmen with no one the wiser.

Once he had Brianna out of the keep, he placed her within the enchanted room he'd created near the Kelpie Ring. He placed a cloaking spell along its borders to assure no one would see or hear her. She had every comfort to keep her occupied until his return. As he did not know how much of the elixir she'd drunk, the golem left her a small ration of food. He did not want his bride to starve to death. Everything now settled, Braun returned to the keep, stealthily returning to his chambers to continue his charade. He staged the room to look as if Brianna had already come and gone. "Now to lay in wait for my revenge." The golem was at the ready.

CHAPTER 11

Death and Discovery

LAIRD ASHEBORO WALKED into Braun's chamber to see his son. All seemed well. The room smelled of flowers and tea. Braun lay quietly sleeping in his bed, the picture of health. Brianna must have been able to help restore him. He did not want to disturb Braun as he rested. "Perhaps tomorrow we shall speak to my son," the Laird whispered to himself. The Laird did not know that he would never be able to speak to his son, as it was the golem that laid in Braun's bed.

The day came and went throughout the keep. With the arrival of the King it was hard to keep up with the comings and goings of the villagers. Cameron went out into the banquet hall to find his beloved and inquire about her recent patient. As he made his way, he noticed many of the servants were nervous and would not look his way. This behavior became so unnerving, he stopped one of the chambermaids and asked what was amiss.

She dared not look into his eyes. "Sophia, there is nothing to fear. I will not harm you. What has happened?" She looked up into the Lairds' eyes and whispered, "Lady Brianna is missing." Cameron froze in place. He did not realize he was holding tightly to the chambermaid until she began to tug away from him. He immediately let her go.

"I am sorry, Laird Cedar-Kellen. We were strictly told not to say a word." The maid looked petrified for disobeying her Laird. She curtsied quickly and ran away to the kitchens, leaving Laird Cedar-Kellen alone in the hallway. *How could this be, why hasn't anyone told me of her disappearance, are they searching for her?* These were the questions running through his mind as he stormed through the keep in search of Laird Asheboro and Maximus.

Fuming with anger, he finally found the Laird and Maximus meeting with the King. Not wanting to be rude, he attempted to stay calm before breaching the trio's conversation. His temper and agitation could not be contained. "What has happened to Brianna?" The men turned and realized that someone had disobeyed their orders of keeping Cameron in the dark about Brianna's whereabouts.

"Cameron, please steady yourself. We are doing all we can do to locate her," said Laird Asheboro. "She may have completed all of her visits with the sick and gone to her gardens to replenish her herbs, " stated Maximus.

The King explained they had visited Braun and noticed Brianna had already visited him as she left behind a few herbs and tea that had been already taken. Nothing seemed amiss. As they attempted to locate her, it seemed that she was no longer in the keep. "We will find her, do not worry." The King had sent four of his most trusted knights to join the search party.

Cameron hoped with all his heart that they were correct, Brianna had simply slipped away to her gardens and would return before supper. To distract himself, Cameron decided to go for a hunt. He would return with a pheasant or stag to then present it to the King as a gift. Cameron returned to his chambers, changed, and grabbed what he believed to be his bow and arrows. A few men joined Cameron and set out for the forest. The fates were kind to the hunters. The group had only been in the forest for an hour when a glorious stag came upon them. The group was in hot pursuit of the animal. Cameron was primed to take the shot. As soon as the stag entered the clearing, Cameron pulled back his arrow, held his breath and released. The arrow was true to its mark, and the stag fell instantly to the ground.

The group roared with excitement, running to retrieve their prize. Cameron felt exhilarated after the hunt. He could not wait to return to the keep and see his future bride. As he mounted his horse, Cameron began to feel faint. He ignored his symptoms and thought it was from the excitement of the day. As the group began their ride back to the keep, the men noticed Cameron not being able to steady himself on his horse. This was very unlike him. He was a master horseman. Two of King Arthur's knights, Galahad and Gareth, rode on either side of Cameron to watch over him. As they came closer to the keep, Cameron grew weaker. His skin became pale and his breathing labored. "My Laird, what is the matter?" asked Galahad. Cameron could no longer focus, and the world seemed to be spinning.

"I know not what is happening to me. My body feels weak. I no longer have the strength to even raise my head." Growing worried, Gareth rode ahead of the party, hoping he would be able to find Brianna or a healer to help Cameron. The moment Gareth rode off, Cameron slumped in his saddle. Galahad was swift in his actions and was able to prevent Cameron from falling off of his horse. The group was in shock, not knowing what to do. Cameron was barely breathing and motionless. Quickly, the group gathered materials to create a makeshift pallet to place Cameron in. He would not be able to make the journey on his horse. Once all was set, the pace to return to the keep became more hurried, and the men continued to monitor the Laird's health.

Gareth had relayed the events to the King and Laird Asheboro once he arrived. "Has Brianna been found?"

"No," both men replied.

"Perhaps Merlin has arrived by some miracle?"

"No," Arthur replied. "I do not believe Cameron will survive the journey if we do not make haste and find a healer."

"Fear not, Gareth, we will find the remedy and Brianna." Arthur was now becoming uneasy with the events that had transpired in the last several hours. "First Braun arrives and collapses, Brianna disappears, and now Cameron has fallen ill with a mysterious sickness. There is something we are not seeing," Arthur told Laird Asheboro. "We must speak to Braun. He will provide more information of his whereabouts and the people he had encountered."

The hunting party arrived with Cameron motionless. You would have thought he was dead if it were not for the very slight rise and fall of his chest. The men quickly carried him into the keep and directly to his bed chambers. Laird Asheboro and the King followed. Lady Asheboro began to orchestrate the chambermaids and servants. Steaming water was brought in to fill a tub. The chambermaids then added rosemary and peppermint oils to the water in hopes of waking the motionless Laird. The men stripped Cameron of his clothes. Once the tub was ready, they lifted him into the healing waters to see if he would rouse. Nothing happened.

Lady Asheboro then brought a tincture of ginseng with honey to gently drop into the young Laird's mouth. Nothing still. The group grew more concerned when nothing seemed to take effect on Cameron. He was removed from the tub and placed into his bed. Lady Asheboro instructed them to continue with the tincture every few hours until a healer could come. Jada offered to stay with the fallen laird to monitor his illness. Once every-one had left the bedchamber and only Jada and Maximus remained, they began to combine their powers to see if they could magically heal the young Laird.

Maximus knew Merlin was on his way. If they could not help, he would be able to assist. Jada gently placed her hands on Cameron's chest. She could feel the faint rhythm of his heart and shallow breaths he took. She was not sure if he would remain in this state or progress to something worse. Jada was not the healer Brianna was, but she could slow the process with Maximus' help. Jada took a deep breath and began to probe Cameron's mind. His mind was active, even though his body was not. She saw images of the hunt, him running, pulling his bow and arrow, then striking the stag. His mind then went dark and a new image appeared. Dancing, a festival, and Brianna. She was seeing his memories, from his childhood to the meeting with their families. Nothing was amiss. Jada was truly perplexed by his state. Logically there was no reason for him to be ill. Maximus stepped in and tried to see if he could see more. He began to gently wipe at Cameron's forehead, then proceeded to his chest and ended the ritual at Cameron's feet. He saw the same visions as Jada. Nothing seemed to be out of place. Maximus resolved himself and told Jada, "We must wait until Merlin arrives. He will be able to guide us. Let us turn our focus on locating Brianna. There have been too many things amiss for her to be gone for so long. Even if she evaded her escorts, Brianna would not worry us in this manner." Both agreed to send their sons to search for Brianna.

Once they finished settling Cameron they would meet with River and his brothers. He would then create a strategic plan to search for their youngest daughter.

The couple began to clean the bedchamber and wrap Cameron in the bed sheets. As they were settling Cameron into his bed, his right hand moved slightly to touch Maximus.

Maximus felt a shock and jumped back. He returned to Cameron and once again touched the young man's right hand. Maximus felt the jolt once more but did not let go.

The Ailey patriarch was disoriented by the vision. He saw a bow and arrow, then Braun, then the Kelpie Ring came into view. Maximus gasped when he saw Braun speaking to someone through the Ring. At first he thought it was a water sprite, but then the true nature of the figure emerged. It was Stygian! He had not escaped Solasta but was able to use his magic in the mortal realm. The vision continued. Maximus witnessed the exchange of a bow and arrow along with an ornate bottle with a liquid inside. Next he saw Braun arrive at the keep with the items. Then all went dark once again. There must be something about the bow and arrow. We must search Braun's chambers. Jada stayed by Cameron's side while her husband organized the search of the keep.

Asheboro Forest, Sunset

Merlin and Arthur's Knights were a short distance from the keep. Not wanting to travel in the dark, the group decided to camp and enjoy the beautiful surroundings. Merlin had heard stories from the traveling minstrels of this place. Beauty surrounded them. Everything was lush and green, the smells of earth and rain danced in the air. As the knights made camp and began to settle for the evening, Merlin could feel strong magic all around them. There was something hidden among them, and he could not place his finger on it. There was magic, and it was heavily fortified. Grabbing his staff, Merlin began to slowly walk through the camp. He checked every tent, knight, and horse. Nothing. *This is so strange. I can feel the magic but cannot locate its origins*, Merlin thought to himself.

He spread his search wider and asked Sir Percival to follow. Merlin was able to defend himself but wanted to assure Arthur's men would be warned if something went amiss. As the duo continued their search of the forest they finally came to the Kelpie Ring. Merlin gasped with astonishment when he saw the enchanted portal. It had been 50 years since he had crossed the portal entrance into the mortal world. He'd left his family and friends without a single word. His heart had broken when he'd made the decision but he knew if he wanted to save Solasta and the mortal realm he had to try and change their fate. How could he have forgotten its location?

Sir Percival was enchanted by the beautiful gems and stones that adorned the Ring. Merlin warned him to not touch a single stone for it may be charmed to cause harm. Merlin inspected the Ring. There were new runes drawn upon it. The Ring no longer allowed free passage and was sealed from the mortal side. The magic that pulsed from the waters was intoxicating. Merlin was tempted to siphon its powers. He thought better to leave it until he was able to discover why it was so heavily protected.

As Merlin continued his inspection, he realized that the protective spell was slightly weakened and that a darker magic was seeping through. Sir Percival continued to be entranced by the sparkling cool pool and could not fight the temptation to have a small taste from its waters. Before Merlin could stop him, Sir Percival was dipping his hands into the waters and drinking the sweet cooling liquid. The pool immediately began to change colors and a mist slowly rolled in.

Sensing there was danger, Merlin placed a protective spell on Sir Percival and himself. Wanting to see what would happen, Merlin cloaked himself to observe. He knew Sir Percival was in no danger with his protective spell. The knight began to speak as if a person was standing in front of him. As the mist began to dissipate, Merlin could see that a mirage was being projected in front of the knight. Dark magic was truly being used. Merlin looked closer as the mirage began to change. The figure no longer was a beautiful water sprite but Stygian. The dark King had somehow found a way to communicate in the mortal realm.

This must be why the Kelpie Ring was so heavily enchanted. Someone has entrapped the Dark King in Solasta. Merlin's thoughts were swirling. This meant his prophecy was beginning. *Stygian has destroyed Solasta and has been sealed from the mortal realm.* Merlin knew he had to reach the keep immediately. There was no time to waste. Merlin did not want to show himself and remove the element of surprise. Sir Percival was so jovial and the water sprite enticing.

The illusion began to reach out to the knight, and Merlin chuckled to himself. He knew the illusion would be broken once "she" touched the knight.

As the sprite's slender hand reached out to touch Sir Percival, there was a faint buzz that electrified the air. The moment she touched, him the true nature of the sprite was revealed and Sir Percival was awakened from the trance. He immediately drew his sword to fight the grotesque creature that stood in front of him. Stygian was tricked and now the entire group would be alerted. A flash erupted between Stygian and Sir Percival.

Once he was able to look, Merlin saw the knight on the ground motionless and Stygian's image gone. Quickly, Merlin went to the knight and checked that his protective spell had deflected the magic Stygian produced. Sir Percival was stunned by the impact but safe. In haste to protect and remove the knight, Merlin almost missed the odd cocoon laying only feet away from him.

Before he could investigate the object, he wanted to assure that Stygian was gone, at least for now. Without removing his cloaking enchantment, Merlin went to the edge of the Kelpie Ring. Gently he placed his hands on the stones and closed his eyes. As he began to channel the energy from the Ring, Merlin received a vision. At first it was Stygian speaking to a young man, then the man being cocooned, followed by the creation of a mud doppelganger of the young man. The vision then faded. A new vision followed. The mud creation was leaving the Kelpie Ring in the direction of the keep, looking disheveled and carrying with him a bow with arrows and an elaborately decorated bottle with a liquid inside.

"Damn! We must leave now. Everyone is in danger." Merlin slowed his thoughts to focus on the young man inside the cocoon. Not wanting to leave the young man behind, Merlin hoped beyond all hope he was still alive. Sir Percival was beginning to awaken from his shock. He steadied himself and made his way to the mage. Merlin placed his hands on the cocoon. He could sense only the slightest essence of life within its fibers. He began to speak an incantation to hopefully release the captive inside.

"Web of desire, web of darkness, release your captive. Tendrils Intertwined, loosen your hold. Come into the light gentle sleeper and awaken."

The earthly cocoon began to unravel. Vines began to release and snap, revealing the unknown man lying in the center. He was cold as ice. He must have been encased for several days. Merlin did not know that the mud creation was linked to Braun. Once he removed the enchantment from Braun, the mud creation was dissolved. The magical link Stygian had with his mud doppelganger was now severed.

Merlin told Sir Percival to quickly rouse the men and break camp. "We must leave within the hour." Percival at first did not understand the urgency in Merlin's request. "Percival, our King and the Laird we are visiting are in mortal danger. If we do not leave now, their fates may be sealed forever." Percival knew to never disregard King Arthur's mage.

He quickly ran to his men and they prepared to leave. Merlin removed the rest of the young man's confines.

Once the captive was free from his bonds, Merlin knew it would only be moments before the young man would take his last breaths. Braun regretted all he had done. He was fooled by the sprite and blinded by his vengeance. With the last moments of his life, he looked to his savior and said, "Please tell my father I am sorry. The fate I have succumbed to is most deserved. I ask for his forgiveness." Merlin knew these were the last words of a dying man and tried to console him the best he could. "My dear boy, I will tell your father. Who do we relay the message to?" In that moment Braun took his last breath and was finally at peace. Merlin never learned of who to find, but he would not allow the young man's words to be said in vain. The mage proceeded to prepare the body for transport to the keep. He did not want to leave him without finding his loved ones and providing a place of rest. Once Merlin completed his ablution, he enchanted the body to float alongside him, wrapped it in fine linens, and proceeded to lead the knights to Asheboro Keep.

CHAPTER 12

Merlin

SINCE THE DISAPPEARANCE of Brianna and Cameron falling under a strange curse, the keep was unsettled. The Ailey brothers had yet to locate Brianna. River used his powers of flight to scan the lands from above but could not see any sign of her. Rune and Ronan had a group of fae, including Echo and his fast-flying fairies to search by ground. The abilities of Echo's team of fae was remarkable. Due to their speed, they were able to cover twice the distance of any other fae. If there was any sign of attack they would be able to combine their powers to create destructive tornadoes. These abilities, along with those of Ronan, who could control the weather, would release a maelstrom that no one would be able to survive. Watchmen were placed throughout the battlements, with everyone taking shifts to rest. Jada and Maximus waited to hear word from their sons on locating their youngest daughter.

As Merlin and his men approached, they could see torches lit along the battlements.

One of the knights noticed a small glow in the distance, followed by a few more torches. He became nervous, sounding the alarm. At once the entire keep was on full alert. Clansmen and knights all rushed to the portcullis and battlements. They were ready for any intruder that would dare come in the cloak of darkness. A voice began to call out from the approaching group. "We come in peace," yelled the voice. "We bring you Merlin the Mage." Everyone at the keep took a deep breath.

It was worrisome that the group did not stop to camp for the evening. Once the men arrived, Merlin announced himself. "My King, it is I, Merlin, your advisor and friend. Please allow entry, for I have much to tell you that cannot wait." Both Laird Asheboro and King Arthur ordered for the portcullis to be lowered and the keep made ready for the new arrivals. The knights set up camp once again in the bailey, while Sir Percival escorted Merlin inside to meet with King Arthur. Merlin did not want to bring in the poor soul that had died in the cocoon until after he had spoken with the King and Laird. He asked for a cart to be brought out to him before he entered the keep. Once the cart arrived, Merlin arranged the young man in it and covered him once again. Hopefully he would be able to find the family of the deceased to allow a proper burial.

"Merlin! How did you arrive so quickly?" Arthur exclaimed as he greeted his dear friend.

"I felt a pull to this keep once you left us in Perth."

"Of course you did; my advisor knows all. Forgive my rudeness—let me introduce you to our host, Laird Asheboro." The group finished their introductions. Arthur could see in Merlin's demeanor that there was something of concern to discuss. After the knights were fed for the evening and settled, the King, Merlin, and Laird Asheboro quietly retreated to the King's chamber to discuss Merlin's concerns.

"Merlin, tell us what weighs on your thoughts. Why have you come in such haste? We are thankful for your arrival, because one of our Lairds has been struck by an illness we cannot seem to treat." Arthur and the Laird gave Merlin the details of Cameron's state and the disappearance of Brianna. They did not know if the incidents were connected. "Also, my son, Braun, was accosted in the forest and arrived in a state of exhaustion and only requesting water. Brianna was the last to treat him," interjected Laird Asheboro.

Merlin's interest piqued with the mention of the Laird's son. "Your son only requests water? No sustenance?"

"Yes, the last we checked on him he was resting in his chambers. All of Brianna's tinctures and herbs were left by his bedside table."

"Let us check on him, for I fear there may be darker forces at work here," Merlin replied. The trio quickly went to the west wing of the keep, entering Braun's chamber. Merlin knew the moment he walked in that the young man in the cart was the Laird's deceased son. Laird Asheboro looked horrified at the bed. The room was as they had left it an hour earlier with one macabre difference. In the center of the bed laid a grotesque malformed body. Merlin was the only one to move closer to inspect the oozing dark mass. He covered his nostrils to not be offended by the emanating stench. Merlin knew exactly what lay before him.

"My dear Laird, your son never came to the keep. What arrived was a golem enchanted to look as your son. The remnants that you see are of the dark magic that created him from the earth surrounding the Kelpie Ring." Both the King and Laird Asheboro stood in shock at the revelation. All this time, they had thought it was Braun in the keep. They both immediately began to ask questions. "How did this happen? Who would do this to a family and village? Who could possess such powers?"

"One moment, gentlemen," Merlin said. "We must first contact Brianna's family. If this golem was sent to harm the keep and your family she is in grave danger."

Too many things were beginning to unravel for the Laird. He thought his son was in the keep, now he was a golem. Then Cameron was under some magical sleep following Brianna's disappearance. *What will come next?* he thought. "Whoever has dared to curse our clan will pay with their flesh!" Laird Asheboro roared with anger.

Merlin was pensive and did not want to upset the Laird further, but he knew he had to reveal the horrific truth that the Laird's son was deceased. Arthur once again noticed Merlin's demeanor. He knew there was more to the story, and Merlin was attempting to soften the blow. The mage took a deep breath to steady himself and began to recount what he encountered in the woods. "As our group approached your lands, we found the enchanted Kelpie Ring. I warned the men to not partake of its waters, but Sir Percival drank from it and was enchanted. I searched the Ring and encountered a strange cocoon. After receiving my vision from the stones around the Ring, I released the young man from the ensnared cocoon. Unfortunately, the young man did not survive being untethered from the golem. We have brought him to the keep to locate his family," Merlin continued. "I know now who the young man is."

"Tell us, by God, so that we may contact his family and prepare his burial ceremony" Laird Asheboro said anxiously.

"My Laird, the young man we brought back is your son." Merlin paused for a moment before continuing to explain how his son was murdered. "Being encased in the cocoon, Braun was deprived of food and water. The magic that was used continually drained his life force to maintain the golem. The cocoon was the connection to the person who was controlling the golem physically and mentally. When I released Braun from his cocoon, the enchantment was broken, severing the connection between the person who was controlling the golem and the life force maintaining the creature. Hence, the oozing grotesque mass now lying in Braun's bed."

Laird Asheboro was stunned. He could not speak. He sat in the room silently, motionless, with a blank stare. Merlin looked to Arthur for assistance, but Arthur was just as taken aback by the revelations. Once he could compose himself, Arthur moved toward Laird Asheboro. He laid a gentle hand on his shoulder. "We will avenge your son." Knowing the loss of a child is unfathomable, Arthur did not want to cause more heartache. "We have learned much from Merlin. Laird, go to your wife and be consoled that my knights and Merlin will not rest until we have restored safety within your lands and the kingdom."

Laird Asheboro, stunned by all the news, simply nodded his head, rose, and began to leave the chamber. Once the shock of the moment passed Laird Asheboro turned to the two men in the room. "Thank you for bringing my son back home and for your willingness to avenge his death. We must now think of Brianna and Laird Cedar-Kellen."

In the wee hours of the morning, all the men met again and summoned Maximus. They needed a plan on how to locate Brianna, cure Cameron, and stop the malignant Stygian. Merlin knew much would need to be explained once Maximus arrived. No one in the Asheboro Clan knew that the Ailey family or the village for that matter were all fae. The Laird may need some time to understand why the village had never revealed their true nature.

Ailey House

Celeste ran into her parents' home, holding her amulet. Tears were streaming down her face. She did not know how to compose herself. "She has been murdered!" Celeste screamed. "Who would dare kill my beautiful baby sister? By the gods, why!" Celeste was inconsolable. Both Jada and Maximus ran to her as she collapsed to the ground. The beautiful amulet that once only held one gem now had two with an additional leaf. Maximus grew concerned, for he created the amulets to seek each other if ever the owner no longer drew breath. "This cannot be. Brianna is well and we will find her. Let me see your amulet," Maximus gently spoke.

The moment Celeste's necklace touched his hands, it began to vibrate. There was strong magic tied to it, and it was not his. Maximus continued to examine the amulet and saw a minuscule drop of blood on the emerald. He gently placed the necklace on the table. "Quickly locate our village and clan map. Only Brianna would have used blood magic to assist in her rescue." Maximus pricked his finger to activate the hidden magic and placed a single drop on the emerald to combine with Brianna's.

Jada placed the village map down first. Maximus held the amulet above the map and hoped it would place itself on her location. Nothing. The amulet would not move. Jada removed the map and began to place the clan map. Before she could finish laying out the contents, the amulet began to move and swing. Slowly Maximus moved his hand methodically over the map. The amulet pulled to the location of the Kelpie Ring and began to spin. The locator spell worked.

As the amulet began to whirl, the enchantment Brianna placed on it began to sing.

> *"Blood of my Blood, giver of life, I now journey to the river of death. Blood of my Blood, life after death, may my journey be*

calm and light. Blood of my blood, the River Styx, the ring will forever be my peace and sight."

Maximus knew where she was and who had taken her. Looking up at his wife, "She is alive, but Stygian has her."

"It cannot be, how has he come to the mortal realm?"

"I do not believe him to be here, yet. He has somehow taken Brianna to the Kelpie Ring. We must go to the Laird and King. The mortal world is in danger, and if Stygian is able to release himself from Solasta, all will be lost." Maximus instructed his wife to gather all their children. Once he returned, he would explain the plan to the village.

They first would have to reveal their secret to the Laird and hope he could overlook the betrayal of their people's origins.

Solasta

Stygian believed all was well. He had cocooned Braun, created the golem to replace him, and enchanted both Brianna and Cameron. His plan was moving along swimmingly and nothing could stop him now. Once he was able to break the enchantment on the Kelpie Ring, he would be able to enter the mortal world and begin his reign of destruction. The moment Stygian was done with his golem, he would release Braun from his snare and allow fellow hunters to find his body. The Dark Fae King finally slept well after his golem retrieved Brianna from the keep.

No one would ever find her hidden within the Kelpie Ring. To free Brianna from her current prison would mean the destruction of the Kelpie Ring enchantment. He had the sole power to free her, or so he thought. Stygian arose the following morning rejuvenated and ready to deploy the next part of his plan. He needed the golem to lure someone from the village to the Ring. Once there, he would be able to probe their mind and see how he could break the enchantment holding him prisoner in the fae world.

Stygian did not have much time left, as his powers were growing weak. The few fae who stayed behind as his army could no longer produce enough food to maintain their forms. Slowly Stygian began to place each weakening fae into a crystal to preserve their powers for himself. Solasta was quickly diminishing into darkness. The animals were dying from the lack of vegetation and the waters no longer ran clear. The dark magic was consuming their realm. Stygian needed to escape. He watched Brianna constantly. She was a clever fairy. Learning from her experience with his golem, she refused the provisions he left for her. He had hoped to soon be released from Solasta and take her as his bride, but something now seemed out of place.

By luck, another weary traveler passed by the Kelpie Ring. He drank from its waters, giving Stygian the opportunity to probe his mind. It was a knight. *He will be very useful,* Stygian thought to himself. He entered the knight's mind, learning King Arthur was in residence at the keep. There was a group of knights heading there to deliver a message. "Why can I not see more? There has to be more than a simple group of knights traveling to the keep." Suddenly, the trance ended and Stygian lost the knight. "How were my powers thwarted?" He now knew there was something afoot. He began to reach out to his golem to gather more information. He rummaged throughout the chamber to see if there was anything amiss. Then he began to hear voices. It was the Laird and King Arthur. There was a third voice but he could not recognize it.

He quickly returned to the bed so that he could overhear their conversation and learn the identity of the third person. Once settled, Stygian heard the door to the chamber begin to open. He saw the Laird and the King emerge first. The third figure was just about to come through the door. He could only see a hand at first and noticed a beautiful signet ring set with a ruby and a letter M. *I need more*, Stygian said to himself.

As he continued to search for the third figure, Stygian began to lose his control over the golem. He took a steadying breath to absorb more power from his crystals. When he tried to reach his doppelganger again, he could not sense it. There was no essence of Braun to tether to, either. "What happened to his connection? Was he found and the keep is now on high alert?" Stygian became frantic. He needed to expedite his plans and break free from Solasta before Maximus and the village realized he had been able to get through the weakened enchantments.

CHAPTER 13

We Are the Solasta Fae

IT HAD BEEN years since he had seen his brother and village. Merlin did not know how Maximus would receive him. King Arthur, Laird Asheboro, and Merlin conversed in the banquet hall as they awaited Maximus.

"I know where Brianna is," exclaimed Maximus as he entered the banquet hall, completely forgetting about social graces. "Forgive me my King and Laird." He slowly bowed and waited to be addressed.

"No need to be so formal, Maximus. My mage has told me much about you and your family. We are equals here." Laird Asheboro looked at the King in confusion and wondered why he would address Maximus in such a way. King Arthur then addressed Laird Asheboro. "You see, Laird Asheboro, in my Kingdom we are all men of flesh and bone. There is no one who is above all others. Camelot embraces the ideology of the round table. I may be the King, but I would not be able to rule if I were not just to my people."

"Thank you, your highness. Please forgive my confusion. Your reign shall forever be of light and justice. May Camelot always stand."

In his rush, Maximus did not realize there was another person in their group waiting to be acknowledged. He slowly turned to see his older brother, Merlin. "How can this be? I thought you were lost to us for all eternity after you left the council!" Tears began to well up in Maximus' eyes. The brothers embraced and time stood still for just a moment for them to enjoy their reunion. Merlin then spoke to his brother. "Maximus, I will explain all once we have resolved our current situation. Believe me when I say the hardest thing I ever had to do was sacrifice my ties to my family to assure our future." Once they were able to collect themselves, they focused their attention onto Laird Asheboro. "There is a story we must tell, Laird Asheboro. But we do not have much time, for I have located Brianna. It is imperative that we create a plan to save her. Merlin, dear brother, can you assist me as you once did when we were children?

"Of course." Merlin placed his hands on his brother's shoulder. "King Arthur, Laird Asheboro, please join your hands with mine." The men looked skeptical but did as Maximus requested. Instantly, images began to flood their minds. Fae were being murdered or tortured, the Ailey family running as dark fae gave chase. Stygian collecting fae powers into his many crystals. The last image they were left with was Maximus being tortured by Stygian as his family and village escaped Solasta into the Scottish Highlands.

The King and Laird Asheboro slowly opened their eyes to look at the brothers. They were completely astounded by the events they were shown. Merlin continued, The stories you heard as a child from your nurse maid and governess were true stories of our land and people. They themselves were perhaps fae, hoping to pave the way for future generations." Laird Asheboro was astounded. All the stories he had heard as a child were true, and not fantasies with colorful characters and whimsical adventures.

"This explains so much. I wondered how your village was so prosperous."

"My dear Laird, please know we only used our powers when necessary. We never used them for ill will or vengeance. Our people believe in the circle of life. Where there is a beginning there must be an end. When called upon, we will fight, but only to preserve the balance of our realm."

Maximus continued the telling of the fate of Solasta. "This leads us to why we came to the mortal world. Our home was once beautiful. When Merlin left the council and entered the mortal realm, Stygian, a dark fae, came into power. The Elders were frightened of him and never truly opposed his edicts. As his reign continued, the dark magic he continuously used began to corrupt his soul. The hatred he held for the mortal realm ate away at his ethereal being. It became all encompassing. He sought revenge for the lives of his family, and no one could stop him. As Stygian's powers grew, so did his lust for destruction. Because of his dark magic, our world began to deteriorate. The once-clear blue waters became dark and muddy. The crops withered, and the animals could scarce survive. Our people were soon beginning to disappear and villages were destroyed. Our small village was the last stronghold against Stygian and his minions."

Laird Asheboro was astonished by what he was hearing and the bravery it took for Maximus to save his village. He understood now that they were fighting for preservation of their fae way of life. "I see. How do Brianna and Cameron play into all this? And how do we save them? I understand that this fae king wants to destroy the mortal world to slake his dark lust, but why does he need Cameron and Brianna?" "Cameron was a diversion. Brianna, on the other hand, is key to his plan. Before we left Solasta, Stygian was searching for a bride, and he chose Celeste. She was the eldest Ailey female. She would have been able to provide heirs."

Laird Asheboro still looked perplexed. "If Celeste was his original target, how did Brianna become his focus?"

Merlin interjected this time, providing the missing link. "Braun brought Brianna to his attention. He was able to learn of the escaped Luminian fae and where the Ailey family hid."

Maximus continued, "Brianna is a rare talent. Only a few healers are born every generation, and Brianna is the most powerful of her kind. With her powers, she can bring anyone back from the brink of death or ease their passage to the otherworld. Even though her talent is healing, our family is able to share our gifts with each other and amplify our strength."

Laird Asheboro's eyes grew wide. "So, this means she would have been able to tap into her family's powers to amplify her own?"

"Yes, which is why we must make haste to find her", Maximus replied.

"She would be a most fearsome creature to behold, for she would be able to kill in an instant with a mere glance?" Laird Asheboro exclaimed.

"You are correct, which is why we had to leave Solasta. All my daughters hold very powerful gifts. They would do anything to protect us and our village. Stygian knew this. He would have forced them to do his bidding and destroy the mortal world." Maximus felt the burden of his secret lifted as he spoke to the Laird.

There were no more secrets between them. The fear he once had of the Laird discovering their origins dissipated instantly. He could now focus on the task at hand. They must save Brianna and Cameron.

CHAPTER 14

The Rescue

MAXIMUS REMOVED THE amulet he had hidden in his jerkin along with the map of the Laird's lands. "I know where Brianna is," Maximus stated. "She may be in a trance or unable to escape. Before she was taken, she used her powers and blood magic to send her amulet to her sister." Maximus laid the map out and held the amulet above it. Instantly the amulet began to sway and land in the forest near the Kelpie Ring. Once the amulet touched the map, it began to sing.

> *"Blood of my Blood, giver of life, I now journey to the river of death. Blood of my Blood, life after death, may my journey be calm and light. Blood of my blood, the River Styx, the ring will forever be my peace and sight."*

"Brianna must have known somehow that Stygian was her kidnapper and that he would take her to the Kelpie Ring. To ensure her powers would not fall into his hands, Brianna siphoned her magic into the amulet. Once he realizes she no longer can use her magic, she will be in tremendous danger."

Maximus waited a moment for everyone to process the gravity of the situation.

"What of Cameron?" asked the Liard. "How will we be able to help him?"

Merlin interjected at this moment and explained the current enchantment Cameron was under. "Cameron has been spelled with a multilayered sleeping spell. Traditionally, these spells can be broken with the object that was used to tether the enchantment to the individual. We must find the artifact to analyze the extent of the spell. To assure his health, we must continue to feed him hearty broths. If a person is under the spell for too long, they will begin to deteriorate and eventually succumb to the enchantment."

The group sat quietly for a few moments to absorb all that had been discussed. The Laird was still in awe of the new knowledge that was bestowed upon him but was the first to speak. "If we know where Brianna is then let us create a hunting party and go after her."

Merlin thought for a moment before responding to the Laird. "A hunting party will not do. We do not know how strong Stygian is. We must have the element of surprise on our side. He already knows the village of Luminia was able to escape to the mortal realm. We do not know if he is aware of my arrival." Merlin continued to discuss his plan. If he and Maximus were able to combine their powers along with a few of the fae villagers, they would be able to secure the Kelpie Ring. Once the final details were laid out, the men dispersed to return in an hour with the needed men and supplies.

As King Arthur and Laird Asheboro began to collect their items and men, Merlin and Maximus searched Cameron's room for any possible item that could have caused his curse. The room was emanating a strong dark magic. It seemed as if it was coming from Cameron solely. Maximus told Merlin of the vision and what had transpired. "I have ordered the men who were in his hunting party to bring all of Cameron's belongings from the hunt to his chamber. I could not find anything amiss. His clothing was not cursed, his leather water vessels did not contain any trace of poison or sleeping draft. The venison that was hunted did not cause others to fall ill."

The men finally came to Cameron's bow and quiver, filled with arrows. The moment they touched it, the dark magic unleashed a tremendous bolt of fire, knocking them to the floor. For a moment they were stunned. Once they were able to collect themselves, they noticed the spot where the bow and quiver once laid were now gone, leaving a scorch mark on the stone floor. Their faces were grim, as they knew this spell would take more than what they could do alone. They would need the entire Ailey family to come together to break this curse. If they did not find Brianna soon, Cameron would slowly wither away and leave his mortal body to join the ancestors. Without the bow and quiver, there was no way for Merlin or Maximus to know the true nature of the sleeping curse.

The brothers then focused their efforts on Cameron. His breaths were now becoming more labored. The restorative broths were no longer able to sustain him. "The curse must be broken within the next day, or Cameron will be lost to us all," Maximus lamented.

"I may not be able to break this curse, but I can ease its effects," Merlin told Maximus. Using the herbs in the room left by Jada, Maximus and Merlin joined their powers to create an elixir for Cameron. It would not wake him from his slumber, but it would allow his heart to continue as long as he was provided seven drops per hour. Merlin called for the King to explain the current situation. Maximus called for Jada and his daughters. They were now Cameron's keepers. "Do not miss a dose of the elixir," Maximus urged Jada, for if she or his daughters did, Cameron would not survive the day.

King Arthur had gathered seven of his finest knights to help lead the search for Brianna. Maximus and Merlin joined the group, bringing with them the Ailey brothers and the Rohan family men, as they were the second-strongest family of the fae. Merlin wanted to keep his identity hidden from Stygian to continue to protect their element of surprise. To assure this, he enchanted each knight's mind to be cloaked from Stygian. He did not have to do the same for the fae, as they were immune to the spell.

To avoid any information to be revealed to Stygian, only Maximus would be present with the knights during the initial search, as he was able to cloak his thoughts from others. "Once the group arrives at the Kelpie Ring, each knight will search the area to locate Brianna. Maximus will use his powers to secure the Ring and find the source of the dark magic. If successful, we will be able to seal the portal once and for all, never to worry about Stygian escaping the fae realm."

Merlin looked onto the group and hoped beyond all hope that the words he was speaking were true. Merlin continued to address the group. "If I must, I will reveal myself, and the Rohan family will join me in stopping Stygian. We must be careful and not consume any of the waters in the Ring. As we have learned with Sir Percival, one drop of the water will allow Stygian access your mind and thoughts."

Brianna sat in her gilded cage waiting for any sign of an outsider. *I must be cloaked*, she thought to herself. All manners of creatures passed by her but never acknowledged her presence. She attempted multiple times to free herself from the enchanted room, but a barrier spell had been placed to keep her within its confines. Each time she encountered the barrier it would stun her. Even though she no longer possessed her powers, she was able to use her wits to finally create a perimeter of her current prison.

She realized that any form of dirt or dust would activate the barrier just enough for the illusion to be altered. As she would reveal a new part of her prison, she would mark the barrier with a small mound of dirt. Now that Brianna knew where to step, she no longer feared being stunned unconscious. She was beginning to grow thirsty, but did not dare drink from the leather pouch Stygian had left for her.

Brianna continued to observe her surroundings and noticed just outside of her barriers were dandelions and honeysuckle. If she could only access them, she would be able to have some nourishment.

Stygian did not spare any luxury when he created her cage. She had all a woman would ever want. He provided a luxurious bed filled with down pillows and silks. A vanity with perfumes, brushes, and ornate hair combs. There was even a basket filled with food that would replenish each day. It had been three days since Brianna's last true meal. Scared to consume anything Stygian presented to her, Brianna would scavenge whatever roots she could find within her confine. She knew her father and Cameron would come for her; she just needed to survive long enough for them to find her.

Walking along the perimeter, careful not to touch the barrier, Brianna noticed a small cricket hop into her space. "How did you get in, little one?" No other animal had been able to cross the barrier. Each time they would come near the barrier, the poor animal would be stunned and then wake after a few moments. As she placed the cricket down on the floor, she became curious. The cricket moved throughout her small space and then just as easily as he came in he exited her prison. In shock, Brianna fell to the floor and began to throw dirt at the barrier. Why hadn't she realized this before? The barrier merely floated above the ground; it did not completely close her in.

"Thank the gods!" Brianna exclaimed. She knew how to get out of this prison. She simply needed to manage a way for Stygian not to notice her efforts. First, she needed to eat. Brianna began to dig near the honeysuckles and dandelions. Once she was able to dig deep enough, Brianna began to dig toward the barrier, hoping her theory was correct. It did not take her long to reach the flowers. She slowly slipped her hand in the small hole she dug and reached to the other side to grab the awaiting nourishment. It was not enough to fill her belly, but it would give her the sustenance she needed to escape Stygian's prison.

Stygian visited Brianna every night, always asking the same three questions. "Have you eaten today? Is your chamber to your liking? Will you marry me?" Brianna never wavered in her replies. With each question he asked she replied "No". How could she be happy in her "chambers" without any freedom? To think she would eat or drink anything he provided was laughable after the way he had treated her, controlled Braun, and used him as his puppet to drug her. As to the matter of marriage, even if she weren't already betrothed to Laird Cedar-Kellen, she would never marry such a grotesque and malicious person, who thrived on hurting others and destroying everything she held dear.

Through each interaction, Stygian remained quiet and steadfast. His parting words would chill her to the bone. "As you wish, my future bride." He would then leave her once again. He never came to her in his physical form, but in an idealized version of himself as he once was, handsome, tall, with dark hair. She attempted to touch him and quickly learned it was an illusion created by the mist from the Kelpie Ring. Brianna knew he wasn't strong enough to come through the portal but had enough magic to seep his way into the mist.

Soon Stygian would be coming to visit her. She wanted to be prepared for his arrival. To lure Stygian into a false sense of security, Brianna decided to dress herself in one of the gowns he had left for her in a wardrobe along with a beautiful golden circlet adorned with sapphires and emeralds. She sat at the vanity, careful not to use any of the perfumes or oils. She combed her hair and tried to be as alluring as possible. She rearranged the limited pieces of furniture that she could move to hide her discovery, then proceeded to lay a blanket down on the ground and made herself a picnic with the items Stygian had left for her.

She was a vision to behold and when Stygian arrived to see the alluring Brianna seated on the blanket. Every fiber of his being was aching to touch her delicate skin and consume her in every way possible. He now knew what Braun was experiencing when he could not control his urges around the fair maiden. Alas, he was still locked in Solasta and could not break the enchantment to allow him to cross into the mortal realm. All he needed was for Brianna to drink and eat the food he left for her. She then would be tied to him. He just needed her to take one small bite. Her father would not be able to break the bond, for it was dark magic imbued with blood magic. Only Stygian would have the ability to let her go, and of course that would never happen, for she was the key to his domination of the fae and mortal worlds.

"I see you have made yourself comfortable in your new home," Stygian said to Brianna with a sickly sweet tone.

"I am as comfortable as a caged bird can be," she retorted.

"Now, now, my sweet. We can solve all your problems if you would simply accept my hand in marriage."

"As I have said before, I will never marry you. My family and future clan will find me and rescue me from your clutches."

"My dear Brianna, I did not want to show you this, but your betrothed is not able to rescue you and will soon depart this world."

Stygian could see the fear in Brianna's eyes as he began to create a looking glass with the mist. Slowly an image emerged on the reflective surface showing Cameron lying on his bed, barely breathing. His skin was sunken in and it looked as if death was upon him. Jada appeared in the image along with her sisters. They were gently wiping at his brow and administering a broth of some sort. Tears began to fall down Brianna's cheek. "What have you done to him?" she shouted to Stygian.

"I have only released you from your contract. He is in no pain; slowly he will fall into a deeper sleep and then he will no longer draw breath. I have been kind to him.

He will not know what has transpired and peacefully join his family in the heavens. You do have the power to save him if you wish to know how." Brianna was frightened to ask, for she knew what he would request of her to save her one true love. What would life be if she could not be with Cameron? She may not be able to escape, leaving Cameron to wither away and die. His clan would be devastated and call war upon the Asheboro Clan. Her family would be in danger and their secret past locked away for so many years would be revealed.

"What do you ask in return for Cameron's life?"

"I simply ask a life for a life. I will reverse Cameron's curse if you agree to marry me."

"How will I know you have kept your word? You cannot expect me to trust you."

Stygian thought for a moment; there was no other way to break the curse. "Once you say the two little words 'I do,' he will be released from his curse."

"Then so be it. I agree to marry you. If you are not true to your word, our marriage will not be valid. I request a written betrothal to be presented to my father. He must know I was of sound mind when I made this choice."

"As you wish, my future bride. I will supply you with paper and a quill."

Brianna then asked, "How are we to get this message to my father?"

"I will place the message in the forest near the hunting grounds. The message will be found, I promise you." Brianna was not convinced, but she had to save Cameron.

"So be it," she choked. "Bring me the materials and I will write to my father." Throughout their encounter, Stygian was so mesmerized and focused on Brianna he never once noticed the rearranged furniture or the mounds of dirt she had placed as markers for the barrier.

Brianna was growing impatient and wanted Stygian to leave so that she could begin her escape. Because she looked so alluring, Stygian stayed longer than he should and felt his powers waning. He dominated the conversation, regaling Brianna of his adventures and how they would rule the two realms. He promised he would return the following day with her requested items. "There may be a delay in my return, but that should provide you plenty of time to choose your words wisely. If your father does not acquiesce to my demands and challenges our contract, I will kill Cameron instantly and your beloved will be no more."

Hearing these words, Brianna took a steadying breath and nodded her understanding. She had no intention of following through with this plan and hoped to be safe at Asheboro keep before Stygian returned. Brianna noticed Stygian growing weaker as he prolonged his usual visit.

He would need to recover for several hours before he could attempt to project once again.

The moment he dissipated, Brianna began to search her chamber for anything she could use to help dig her way out of the barrier. The combs that were sitting on her vanity would be perfect. She began to dig as fast as she could. Time was not on her side. Once Stygian recovered from this last visit, he would be back. At any small rustle of movement, Brianna would startle, thinking Stygian had returned for one more conversation. The sun began to set for Brianna; it seemed she had been working for hours and made no progress. *This is futile,* she thought to herself. How would she ever make the hole deep enough for her to get through? Her arms were aching and her hands were bleeding from the cuts caused by the hair combs. Still, she could not stop. Her entire world was in jeopardy.

The men were prepared. Maximus and Merlin led the group of knights and fae into the forest. They needed to move quickly, for the sun would begin to set soon and they would lose the daylight. If it was possible, they wanted to refrain from using any magic until it was absolutely necessary. Stygian may know his golem was destroyed but not that they were in pursuit of Brianna. The group traveled with minimal supplies to avoid alerting any of Stygian's minions or magical traps. The Kelpie Ring was a short journey from the keep. Once they reached their destination, the men made camp. Merlin and the Rohan fae stayed behind.

Maximus and each knight were given a small, enchanted bean. Merlin explained if anything were to go wrong to simply swallow the bean and it would transport them back to the camp. This would in turn set the alarm for Merlin and the fae to join in the fight. He warned all the men to not drink from the alluring waters of the Ring. This would alert Stygian that a traveler had discovered the Ring and remove the element of surprise. Maximus would take the lead and guard the Ring, while the men searched throughout the area. Based on the location spell Maximus used, Brianna should be only feet away from the Ring itself.

The Kelpie Ring seemed to shimmer as the sun began to go down. Each gem reflected the suns' rays, creating a kaleidoscope of colors within the forest. Maximus positioned himself to guard the Ring for the knights to search for Brianna. "Remember men, we are not to touch the Ring or the waters." The group began their search. Maximus could sense there was dark magic near the Ring but dismissed it, thinking it was coming from the portal itself. "Men, be on your guard. There is dark magic all around us." Brianna jumped with excitement when she saw her father and the knights. "Father, I am here! Father, Father, I am in front of you." Brianna's voice was becoming hoarse from her efforts. No one acknowledged her. "Damn it!" she exclaimed. "How do I get them to see me?" Brianna began to dig more vigorously and attempted to create a large enough hole to be able to yell for help. The knights sensed there was something amiss but could not explain why.

The search continued as the sun was beginning to set. Brianna was exhausted. She was frightened to attempt to break the barrier as it may alert Stygian that she was trying to escape. She no longer cared what the consequences were; she was getting out of this prison one way or another. She may no longer have her powers, but she still had her fae blood, which held magical properties. She used one of the hair combs to prick her finger. She smeared the ruby liquid all over the hair piece and prayed to the gods that it would be enough to break the illusion for a moment. Brianna waited with bated breath for a knight to turn in her direction. Her father was only mere steps away; he would be able to help her once they knew where she was.

Sir Percival returned to the Ring to speak with Maximus. "I feel as if I am being watched, Maximus. She has to be here." Maximus closed his eyes and tried to focus on his daughter and the amulet. He knew she was close, why couldn't he see her?

"Sir Percival, the dark magic seeping from the Ring seems to be much stronger near the actual entrance to Solasta. Go to the arched bridge." Sir Percival did as he was told. Slowly he walked the edge of the Ring trying to see any disturbances that would reveal Brianna to them. As he walked closer to the bridge he began to notice fresh earth had been moved. Perhaps an animal foraging. He stopped for a moment to look around.

Brianna saw the young knight. He was staring right at her without even knowing it. She took her chance and threw the comb at the barrier. The comb struck the invisible shield and for a short moment flickered. She thought the knight saw her but he still stood frozen in place. Brianna ran over to the comb and once again smeared more blood on it. She needed something larger than a comb to launch at the barrier. She collected the baskets in her chamber and smeared blood onto them as well. Then the torrent of objects hitting the barrier began.

Sir Percival stood frozen in place. For a moment he thought he saw someone flicker in front of him. It was so brief, he was not sure if it was his imagination. He stood staring at the same spot to see if it would happen again. Suddenly, there was a basket in midair with a maiden standing in the background. Then the images disappeared once again. He began to move toward what he was seeing. There was a continuous flicker of objects flying and a maiden for short moments. Sir Percival was intrigued by this phenomenon. He walked closer to the mirage he continued to see and out-stretched his arm. Perhaps he would be able to break the illusion. He then saw complete terror in the maiden's face as he reached toward her. The knight had no idea why she would have such fear; he wore the crest of the King. He held no weapon for attack. Then everything went dark.

Brianna was elated that her attempts at breaking the barrier were working. The knight noticed her. For a moment he looked as if he could not believe what he was seeing. Then he started to move toward her. She was completely terrified. If he were to touch the barrier, it would stun him, dashing her hopes of being found. She still did not know if Stygian would be alerted due to her constant interference with the barrier. She tried to warn the knight, but it was too late. He continued to walk toward her with his outstretched arm. Before the knight knew it, he was on the ground, stunned by the barrier's magical charge.

Maximus quickly turned when he heard something fall to the ground. He called out but there was no response. Walking in the direction of the bridge, Maximus saw a body on the ground. It was Sir Percival. He'd been attacked. Quickly, Maximus called out to the other knights to come to his aid. Sir Lamorak was the first to arrive to assist Maximus. "Take him back to Merlin. I will stay here until the others arrive." As Sir Lamorak took Sir Percival, he instructed the rest of the knights to be on their guard, as there was an evil among them. Sir Gawain and the rest of the knights surrounded Maximus.

"What should we do?" asked Sir Gawain. Maximus thought for a moment. He'd sent Sir Percival in this direction because the dark magic was strongest, yet there was nothing that proved it was not coming from the Ring itself.

Brianna stood frozen, horrified by the effects of the barrier on the knight. She then heard more voices breaking her trance. "Men, hurry. Sir Percival has been injured." It was her father; he had found her deciphering the message. More knights then followed. *One last time*, she thought to herself. Her body was beginning to grow faint from her exertions. Gathering the baskets once again, Brianna waited for the perfect moment to unleash her assault on the barrier.

Maximus thought he saw his daughter but it seemed as if she were a ghost. He continued to look into the forest. Again she appeared in front of him and then was gone. This was the magic he was sensing. She was hidden under a cloaking spell!

"Sir Galahad, go quickly to Merlin. Tell him we have found Brianna. I will need his assistance in removing the cloaking spell and hopefully find a way to remove the barrier that has her imprisoned." He could no longer see his daughter, but he spoke to her. "My darling Brianna, I am here. We have seen you. Hold on for a few more moments— we will release you from your prison as soon as Merlin arrives!"

Sir Lamorak made it to Merlin and explained what had transpired. The Rohan family was ready to fight, but Merlin held them in place. "He has simply been stunned. I do not believe there was an attack. If there was, Maximus would have sent a signal or a knight would have used his bean to instantly reach us." Moments later, Sir Galahad arrived and asked Merlin to return with him, for they had found Brianna. "Maximus requests your assistance in releasing Brianna from a cloaking spell and barrier."

"Very well, let us not tarry here."

Merlin and the fae joined Maximus.

"How is Sir Percival?" asked Maximus.

"He has been stunned; he will recover but will be in pain for several days. I left a few of the Rohan fae behind to watch over him."

Maximus nodded in approval. "Brother, can you help me remove the cloaking spell that has Brianna hidden?"

Merlin could sense the dark magic. "I believe the cloaking spell and barrier are all tied to the Ring. If we remove the enchantments, we will also be releasing Stygian from Solasta."

"That is impossible!" shouted Maximus. "The Luminian village created a blood oath to seal the Ring. We would need the blood of each Luminian family to undo the spell."

"It seems that when you traveled from Solasta to Haven Village the enchantment was corrupted. This allowed Stygian to reach the mortal realm and use the magic within the Ring." Merlin continued, "Perhaps we could find another way to release Brianna. As of now, we do not know if Stygian has been alerted to our arrival."

Brianna knew something was amiss as she watched her father and the other man speak. They could not hear her; if she was able to dig enough perhaps she could call out to them. Not wasting a moment she began to dig. Dirt began to fly. Once the opening was large enough she began to call out to them. Both men stopped speaking for they heard a muffled voice. Brianna saw their reaction and continued to call out to them.

Maximus felt something hit his foot. When he looked down it was a small pebble. Then another fell toward him. His eyes followed the small stones and noticed the fresh earth that was being disturbed by some force.

"Father," Brianna yelled out. Maximus realized it was his clever daughter. The enchantment must not penetrate the ground. "Brianna, we are here. We will save you." Maximus and Merlin instructed the men to step back while they attempted to move the earth enough for Brianna to crawl out. Brianna saw the men stepping back. She did the same. Whatever her father and the gentlemen were planning may cause her harm. She hid behind her bed, heart pounding and holding her breath. *By the gods, may this work*, Brianna thought to herself.

Merlin slowly walked around the perimeter of the barrier. "We must be careful and not break the spell,", Merlin began to slowly remove the earth from below the barrier. Maximus did the same on the opposite end. Brianna could see the earth move and a small opening begin to emerge.

The powerful fae were growing concerned as they yelled to each other. The enchantment was being affected by their interference. They yelled to the knights, "Dig, men!" The knights joined in the attempt to free Brianna. She left her hiding spot, joining the efforts. The hole was growing larger, only a few more large scoops and she would be able to crawl out.

"We must hurry, the barrier cannot hold for much longer," Merlin yelled to the group. Brianna thought the hole was large enough for her to crawl through. Carefully not wanting to be stunned, she slid on her belly into the hole. The knights, between flickers, could see what she was attempting. Sir Galahad immediately went to the opening. First a hand emerged, followed by a slender wrist and an arm. Sir Galahad grabbed her outstretched arm and pulled her to safety. Merlin and Maximus immediately stopped their incantation. The earth they were holding back once again returned to its former state.

CHAPTER 15

Last Kiss

GASPING FOR AIR, Brianna collapsed into Sir Galahad's arms. She was exhausted and needed nourishment. Merlin circled the Ring and tested the magic surrounding it. The Kelpie Ring had been weakened further and more dark magic was seeping through. Merlin grew more concerned knowing Stygian could possibly break down the barrier. The group gathered and returned to the camp where Sir Percival was recovering.

Brianna was shivering and could not stop her teeth from chattering. Maximus provided her with a cloak and some pomegranate wine. She drank the wine, allowing it to provide her comfort and warmth. The tremors began to subside, color returning to her cheeks. With each small sip from the leather pouch, she felt as if her life was returning to her. One of the knights offered her a slice of bread, which she devoured within seconds. Her mouth full, she barely chewed as she continued to consume her weight in food. She suddenly stopped. The knights were in awe of her ravenous state.

"What can I say? A lady has been deprived of nourishment. I must regain my strength to return to my love and defeat Stygian." The men began to laugh at Brianna's words and then quickly remembered she did not know of Cameron's current state. Brianna looked quizzically at the men. They'd been jovial just a few moments before. What had she done to bring the party to such a state? Sir Percival was the first to answer her bewildered look.

"My lady, Laird Cedar-Kellen is in a grave condition. We are not sure if he will ever recover. Merlin has performed a counterspell I believe, but I do not know of the intricate details." Brianna now understood the group's mood.

"I am aware that my love is in a dire state. Before you arrived, I was attempting my own escape so that I would not have to marry the villainous and grotesque Stygian." Both Merlin and Maximus looked toward Brianna as she finished her last sentence.

"Child, what do you mean by marry?" Maximus asked. Brianna then began to explain what had transpired between her and Stygian. "Stygian is able to project himself into the mortal realm for short periods of time with the use of his crystals. The longer he remains in our world the weaker he becomes. Once he has depleted his powers, he returns to Solasta to recover. I promised him marriage if he would save my beloved Cameron. I knew my time was limited. If I did not escape or marry him all would be lost. Stygian was to return to Solasta, acquire the materials I needed to persuade you of my actions, and release his curse upon Cameron."

"By the gods, Brianna! Did you actually believe him?" Merlin retorted.

"Of course not. I would be a fool to think Stygian would ever keep his word. I wanted to buy some time. That is why I was digging for my life to escape the prison he had made for me. He wanted to use my powers to gain access to the mortal realm. He does not know that I transferred my powers and his efforts would have been for naught." At the mention of her powers, Maximus slowly pulled out a small necklace and handed it to her. Her eyes began to glisten with tears. He knew what her message meant. He knew that she had transferred her powers to her sister. As he handed her the amulet, both Maximus and Brianna began to recite the same enchantment. Her hands began to tremble and glow. She closed her eyes to focus on the trapped magic within the amulet.

The men watched in awe of the young maiden as the powers contained within the amulet began to transfer once again to their owner. Her powers were magnificent. When Brianna opened her hands, the necklace was now in two pieces. She placed one of the amulets in her father's hand and the other around her neck. She took a deep breath and addressed the group. "Stygian wants to rule both the fae and mortal realms, wanting to avenge his family's deaths carried out by the Maconite clan. Then take me as his bride. Stygian is a strong fae, but only because he has the crystals of the fallen fae woven into a cloak he wears."

"If we can strip him of his crystals and pass the powers on to their familial relatives, he would not be able to access the power again." Brianna continued, "Once Stygian is stripped of his powers, they would then be able to overtake him and remove him from power." The one question she had was how to protect the Haven fae from Stygian and not allow him the ability to take their powers.

Merlin and Maximus remained silent as they contemplated Brianna's words. They were the strongest family in the realm but could not defeat Stygian if he possessed the crystals. The situation was grave, and the men felt its weight. Maximus was the first to break the silence. "Let us return to Asheboro Keep and see how Laird Cedar-Kellen has fared since we departed. We will then hold a council with King Arthur and the Fae families. There will only be but a few precious hours to prepare for Stygian's wrath. Once he discovers that Brianna has escaped, and the enchantment further weakened, he will be on the warpath."

Merlin rose from the circle beginning to speak an enchantment that Brianna had never heard. As he continued the spell, a portal began to emerge. "Men, quickly, follow me." Maximus told the knights. At first the men were hesitant. "We have no time for this foolishness. We must hurry to the keep. This is the fastest way." The entire camp followed Maximus through the inky black portal. Brianna was last to follow.

"How is this possible?" She looked at Merlin.

"There is much to explain, my dear child."

Before walking through the portal, Brianna took a deep breath and entered the darkness in front of her. As she walked she felt a slight resistance and then a hand guiding her. It felt like an eternity had passed before she reached her final destination. Brianna emerged in the banquet hall with the entire keep staring at her. Merlin followed immediately after her, closing the portal.

Once the party was settled and fed, Brianna was taken to see her beloved. She did not know what to expect. As she hesitantly entered his chamber, she first saw her mother and sister seated next to him, administering an elixir.

"Brianna! My child!" Jada jumped from her chair, nearly knocking over the elixir Merlin had given her for Cameron. Her arms wrapped around her daughter tightly.

"Mother, I cannot breathe," Brianna managed.

Realizing she was smothering her daughter, Jada released her. "We have been watching over Laird Cedar-Kellen. He has not worsened since Merlin gave us this elixir, but we do not know how much longer he can remain in this state." Brianna looked at her beloved. His cheeks were ashen gray and sunken in. He was slipping away.

His once taut and muscular frame looked weak and frail. Jada explained the regimen to Brianna to allow her some privacy with her love. At first, Brianna sat quietly not knowing what to do. *Should I speak to him of my adventure or perhaps read our favorite book?*. She decided on both. With a cooling towel, she wiped his forehead and spoke of her ordeal. She glossed over the part where she'd agreed to marry Stygian to save him, not wanting to upset his slumber.

Once she was done, she again cooled his forehead and admired his features. Typically, a maiden would not have been left alone with her suitor. She had the privilege of caressing his skin and soaking in every masculine feature.

He was truly beautiful. Even though he was wasting away, he was an Adonis. There had to be a way for her to save him. She was still weak from the transferring of her powers, but she had to try. Closing her eyes, Brianna began to chant an old fae lullaby. The rhythm was slow and melodious. She placed her hands on his chest and slowly pushed the calmness she felt from within toward him, trying to find the illness that was causing this curse.

She searched his aura but could not reach the darkness that was holding onto him so tightly. No longer being able to sustain the spell, Brianna gently raised her hands from his chest, grounding herself. She had never had this experience before. As she looked at her hands, Brianna was angered. "My powers have never failed me. Anyone I ever wanted to save, I could. But, alas this was not an injury or illness but a wicked curse placed on you by Stygian." Tears began to well in Brianna's eyes, slowly rolling down her cheeks. "One day my love, we will be together again." Tears continued to fall from her cheeks as she administered the next few drops of Merlin's elixir into Cameron's mouth. She did not realize as she was caring for Cameron that her tears were mixing with the potion. As the last tear and drop of elixir mixed, Cameron's color began to return. Brianna placed a soft kiss upon his lips and said, "I love you, my dear Laird." Brianna hoped beyond all hope that Merlin would be able to break the curse.

She then began to walk over to the bookshelf and quickly selected their favorite book, Beowulf. Not noticing Cameron's chest beginning to rise and fall as if in a natural slumber, Brianna sat next to the Laird's bed. Perhaps hearing her voice would rouse him. She opened the book and began reading::

> *"And now was the first time For the brave young warrior to withstand such fury, The storm of battle, standing beside his beloved lord."*

As she continued to read, Cameron reached out to her and gently squeezed her hand. The book slipped from her fingers, falling to the floor. Brianna slowly looked up and saw Cameron looking at her with a roguish smile. At that moment Brianna forgot about propriety and leapt from her seat to kiss her beloved.

CHAPTER 16

Calm Before the Storm

BRIANNA COULD NOT contain her excitement and joy. "Cameron! How is this possible? The elixir was meant to sustain you until we could find a cure for Stygian's curse."

"Perhaps it was the individual administering the elixir that made the difference," Cameron responded, still weak. Not wanting to hurt him, Brianna held her control to throw herself once again upon him and shower him with kisses. Of course this would not be proper discourse for a lady. She decided to settle for a simple caress of his face and holding his hand. He looked so weak and frail. He needed true sustenance. Brianna called for her father and a maid. Maximus, thinking the Laird had finally succumbed to the curse, walked in with a somber face expecting to console his distraught daughter.

Brianna met Maximus at the chamber door. She could not contain herself as she pulled her father into the chamber and brought him over to Cameron. Maximus did not understand Brianna's enthusiasm until he reached the Laird's bed. "By the gods, how is this possible?"

Cameron was propped up in his bed, slowly sipping on an herbal tea Brianna had made for him. Shortly after, a maid walked into the room and Brianna asked for her to prepare beef broth, bread, and cheese for the Laird. "Quickly, he must begin to regain his strength," Brianna told the young maid as she left the chamber.

Maximus then turned to Brianna, "Child, what have you done to break the curse?"

"I do not know, Father. I was simply following mother's directions of providing the elixir to Cameron. I did attempt to heal him with my powers, but I could only see darkness consuming his heart. The longer I attempted to reach it the deeper it seemed to go. I began to cry because my powers have never failed me before. I then gave him the elixir." Brianna blushed before she continued the rest of her story. "Once I finished giving him the elixir, I kissed him and professed my love."

Maximus now understood Brianna's pause and blush. He then asked one more question. "Did your tears mix with the elixir?"

Brianna did not know if they had. "I cannot say, Father."

Then Maximus proceeded, "Can you still feel or see the darkness within Cameron?" Slowly, Maximus' concern began to dissipate as he examined Cameron. "If the darkness remains within him, the curse has not been broken and Stygian can still unleash his will upon Cameron." Brianna sat next to Cameron and placed her hands on his chest.

She closed her eyes and began to search for any ailment within the Laird. She could feel his weakness, but did not see any darkness. She moved her hands gently toward his heart to assure herself that the curse had been broken. Light began to emanate from her hands. Cameron could feel the warmth she was transferring to his body. His strength seemed to be returning. He no longer felt as if in a trance. His mind was sharp and his senses returning. Realization dawned upon him that his future bride was touching him. The longer she continued her ministrations, the more intoxicated he became by her scent of roses and lavender.

Brianna finally ended his torture and removed her hands from his chest. She smiled at her father and was elated. "The darkness has dissipated. I can no longer sense it."

Maximus was in complete awe. "By the gods! How is this possible? I have heard of ancient magic that could reverse a curse but never have I seen it performed. Perhaps your healing powers are not only limited to your touch. Your tears, blood, or even kiss could have reversed the effects. My mother once told me that true love could cure all."

Unbeknownst to Maximus and Brianna, her powers had grown due to her love for Cameron. Her healing powers were not limited to her hands but to her very essence. Anyone who came in contact with a single tear or a drop of her blood would be healed. The effects would take time if it was a singular drop. The magic would be magnified if her essence was imbued with her love.

Now that the Laird of Cedar-Kellen was recovering, it was time for Merlin and the rest of the keep to learn of his state. Maximus left the chamber to make the announcement. Brianna stayed behind to assure herself that her eyes were not deceiving her and that Cameron was recovered and no longer in any danger. She still had an unsettled feeling. Stygian was out there and would discover her treachery. The Kelpie Ring was weakened further with her escape.

"All will be well Brianna," she told herself. To calm herself, she took a steadying breath and remembered that she had her father, Merlin, an entire fae village, and King Arthur. There was no way that they could lose. Good always conquered evil, or so she hoped.

It felt as if months had passed, but it had only been a week since the curse was broken. Cameron had completely recovered. With each day, his strength grew more along with his stamina. The keep was prepared for Stygian and his minions to storm the gates of the portcullis, but nothing happened. King Arthur, Merlin, and Maximus held daily council meetings hoping their time would not run out.

They had yet to find a plausible way to defeat Stygian without grave losses. Everyone knew a battle was coming, and with battle there were casualties, but they did not want complete devastation.

The knights of the round table presented ideas. The one flaw was how they would be able to remove Stygian's cloak of crystals. This was the one item that made the dark fae invincible. With a snap of his finger, he could demolish an entire military flank. "How do we subdue him long enough to disarm him?" asked Sir Percival. The council meetings were held day and night. The Ailey sisters along with their mother, Jada, would supply the men with much-needed nourishment. As Brianna walked in, she heard Sir Percival's question. For days she had fought the urge to interrupt their debates, but she knew the answer to their dilemma.

"I am your solution," Brianna said firmly.

The room turned in her direction as she walked slowly to the table with their evening meal. The men, who were ravenous, were not tempted by the succulent feast that was presented to them but rather stared in shock at what they had just heard. "Absolutely not!" shouted Maximus. "You have only been with us a week since your rescue and now you want to return to him as a lamb to the slaughter? I will not agree to this preposterous idea."

Brianna looked at her dear father, knowing how much he loved her and would protect her to the ends of the earth. "Father, magic is on our side. We have King Arthur and his knights, in addition to our family and Merlin. I will be well protected and will have nothing to fear. As I see it, Stygian wanted me for his wife because of my powers. He never once knew that I had transferred them in the last moments before my kidnapping. I will do the same once again to assure my powers do not fall into his hands," Brianna continued to explain to the group. "We shall use his own spell against him, and I will not be in harm's way. As Stygian created a golem of Braun, let us create a golem of me."

The tension within the council was still thick, but the men were beginning to listen. If Brianna would not be in direct harm, the plan may perhaps work.

"Stygian is blinded by his lust for power and vengeance. He would not see our deception until it was too late. My golem will return to the Kelpie Ring and call for his return. He does not know that Cameron has recovered. I know the moment he found my prison empty he would have immediately killed Cameron. The golem would come to plead for Cameron's lifeless body to be returned to the mortal realm, and in exchange the golem would become his bride."

Maximus interjected, "Brianna, this is ridiculous! Once Stygian has who he thinks is you, he will not relent on his want for revenge. He will torture the creature beyond all comprehensible will. Please, dear daughter, understand that I have been there. I suffered for several years until I was summoned to Haven Village. Think of your love, Cameron. Does he not matter in this? Have we forgotten what happened to Braun? He was tethered to his golem and died the moment he was released from the creature."

"My dear father, I am fighting for freedom, our village, and Cameron. Each passing day is a weight upon my shoulders. I do not want to live in fear until my dying day wondering when Stygian will come for us. I have faith, hope, and trust in our allies. We will be victorious. And we have learned a few tricks since all these events have transpired. Merlin can place me in a trance and control the golem. The creature will come bearing gifts for Stygian. The golem will present him with a vial of pomegranate wine laced with all of the family's fae blood. In reality it will be a sleeping potion undetectable by the fae. I will supply a few drops of my very own blood. In theory, if my tears were able to remove the dark curse Cameron was under, perhaps my blood can do the same for Stygian and begin to heal the darkness that has consumed him."

The room fell silent as they contemplated Brianna's proposed plan. Sir Gareth then asked, "Brianna is this wise? What if he sees through our charade? Also, how are we to remove the cloak from Stygian?"

"As fae tradition stipulates, a traditional garb is to be worn during the handfasting ceremony where both betroth-ed are to wear a ceremonial fae wrap enchanted with our families' histories to bond our lives. He will have to wear this robe if the ceremony is to be recognized among the fae. Remember my golem will be the one doing all of this. I will be in a trance being monitored by my sisters and mother.

"During the ceremony, the couple will drink from the same goblet with the pomegranate wine laced with the sleeping potion and my blood. Stygian will be skeptical and will only agree to the ceremony if he knows he can trap me. With our family powers, he can reopen the Kelpie Ring. Once the golem and Stygian fall asleep, the knights, Merlin, and the fae can reveal themselves and locate the cloak. The potion will only last for 30 minutes. Everyone will have to work quickly to find the cloak. He will not leave such an important item in Solasta. The one thing we must be sure not to do is wake me before the cloak is found. If we are not able to locate the cloak, the golem must continue the ruse. Merlin will assure my safety."

The room continued to remain in complete silence, then a slow murmur began as the council discussed the plan Brianna proposed. The plan could work, and if they were able to locate the cloak, they would be able to defeat Stygian and remove him as King of the Fae. The room took a collective deep breath. After an hour of discussion, the council agreed to Brianna's plan. They then began to hammer out the details of the how, the when, and where they would stage themselves for the impending battle. All seemed to be as it should be. Asheboro Keep would be saved, and Haven Village would be free from the darkness that had shadowed them since their escape from Solasta.

Unfortunately, there was one flaw in their plan. Stygian knew that the curse placed on Cameron had been broken, and he was now preparing to enter the mortal realm to bring complete destruction to them all.

CHAPTER 17

Darkness Falls

ASHEBORO KEEP WAS as calm as it could be. Merlin began the preparations for Brianna. Elixirs were being made to assure there was enough for at least a month as a precaution. The Ailey women collected mud from the village to sculpt Brianna's golem. They were talented artists. The creation looked as if it would wake at any moment. Once the golem awoke they would dress her and brush her hair. Jada continued to have a nagging feeling that something was amiss, but could not place her finger upon it. There had been no premonitions between Maximus or Jada, which meant Stygian had been able to cloak his thoughts. This was not a good omen for the group. Without the upper hand, there may be more to lose than just Brianna's golem.

Solasta, Stygian's Castle

Stygian had returned to the Kelpie Ring to find an empty bedchamber. Brianna had somehow escaped his prison. He could sense the enchantment separating him from the mortal realm was greatly weakened. However, she escaped caused the enchantment to be almost obliterated. He could now break the seal without needing anyone to assist him. He was salivating at the thought of destroying the barrier and marching into Haven Village in all his glory. Now knowing he could destroy the enchantment; he needed time to gather his minions and fortify his magic.

Once in the mortal realm, he would demand each villager to bow to him before he crushed their souls and usurped their powers. The vision danced in his mind as a sumptuous buffet of death and power. All the fae dead at his feet with the Ailey sisters bound and enslaved to him. Each becoming his concubine, while their brothers were held in the dungeons barely living to simply be drained of their powers.

Their lives were held to control the sisters. The moment a sister were to deny him, a brother would die. Stygian would save their parents for last. During a banquet in his honor held by a few of the mortals he allowed to survive, Maximus and Jada would be presented to him bound by silver chains. This would inflict intense pain while not allowing them to use their magic. He would summon the Ailey siblings to sit next to him on the dais to watch the festivities and entertainment.

The main event would lead them out of the banquet hall where a massive wood pyre was prepared for their occupants to arrive. As the Ailey siblings followed the crowd chained together, they realized what they will be watching, the death of their mother and father. Oh, the thought of this vision was all-consuming for Stygian. He would have the sisters and their powers, the brothers tortured and drained of their magic, and the crowning event: Maximus and Jada dying in a glorious blaze. Stygian slept soundly for the first time in 20 years.

The next morning, Stygian arose and gathered his minions. They spent a week making preparations to storm the Kelpie Ring. Wearing his cloak, Stygian had the power and enough fae blood to remove the remnants of the enchantment. The dark fae army was small but mighty. They gathered weapons and shields along with food rations. They believed the invasion would only take mere minutes. Arrogance blinded them, as they did not prepare for an extended battle. They only had five horses for the army of 1000, but they were mighty, Black shire horses, with red eyes and long, flowing manes. Simply looking at them one would think they'd come straight out of hell.

Stygian rode on his stallion, Abyss. His two lieutenants rode Tartarus and Nightshade who were equally menacing. The shire horses possessed the power to emanate a shockwave when they stomped their hooves. This would cause anyone in their immediate vicinity to be stunned. They led the army toward the Kelpie Ring, providing an additional layer of protection for the dark army. As the fae followed the fae king, the sky began to darken. Stygian took care to shield his army's minds. This would thwart Maximus from receiving a premonition of their arrival. They had the upper hand, and no one would be able to stop them. "This is our time!" yelled Stygian to his men. "We will have dominion over both the fae and mortal realms. Fear nothing, for I am your King. We hold the power of the ancient families. No one will dare to defy us!" The fae army roared with the banging of their shields and war cries. The men were raging with maddening hysteria and testosterone. Stygian served each fae a concoction that multiplied their senses. They were stronger and quicker, allowing them to focus on their keen sense of sight. The army marched in unison toward the Ring. The closer they got to the Ring, the darker the sky became, followed by thunder and lightning.

Stygian thought it was due to his power, and that nature was heralding the coming of his army's onslaught. Unbeknownst to him, the storm was placed by Merlin through a protective warning spell around the Kelpie Ring to alert the keep if Stygian was on his way to the Ring.

Asheboro Keep

Merlin gathered Maximus, King Arthur, the knights, and Laird Asheboro. With Stygian shielding his thoughts, the keep had been preparing for war the moment Brianna was rescued. The golem was ready, the men had been sparring for the last seven days, and the food rations had been stored. Merlin placed a protective spell on their water supply to assure it could not be poisoned.

The advantage they had was Stygian did not know Merlin was at the keep. Asheboro and Haven Villagers had been moved to be within the keep walls. The people were crowded but safe. Only a few fae men remained in the village as scouts and sentries. They knew the battle would be gruesome and many would lose their lives, but the balance between good and evil had to remain.

The fae and mortal realms needed to be saved from the darkness that was approaching. The keep was continuing its preparations when the clouds began to roll in. The sky was becoming an ominous gray, leading into an inky black. Merlin knew it was time. He watched the skies for a moment and when the first crack of thunder came he immediately went into action. The counsel gathered and listened to Merlin's every word. "Stygian is upon us. As the wind howls and thunder cracks, he draws closer to the Kelpie Ring. We must send out our golem in hopes of slowing him down to allow us time to place magical barriers strong enough to keep his army out."

Jada looked into her husband's eyes, her own filled with tears. "Our sweet child, she will be all right, won't she?" asked Jada to both her husband and Merlin.

Merlin assured her he had taken every precaution to protect Brianna. "The golem is tied to her in spirit only through the dream world, unlike Braun, who was tied to his golem both physically and mentally. If any harm comes to the golem, the enchantment will immediately reverse and Brianna will awaken when the golem loses consciousness." Trusting in the powers that be, Jada went to retrieve her daughter to begin the transition into deep sleep. The Ailey family sealed Brianna, her sisters, Jada, and Guinevere in the bedchamber with provisions. They would be safe until the battle was complete.

The men and knights began to fill the inner bailey preparing for battle. The Ailey brothers were responsible for orchestrating the fae attacks. As the keep buzzed with anxious energy, Merlin gathered King Arthur and Laird Asheboro. The council met one last time before chaos would ensue. Stygian was on his way. Once they began to hear the continuous crack of thunder, they would only have a few moments to steel their nerves before Stygian would arrive in the mortal realm. "Men, this is our time. As the devil reaches our gates, we will be victorious. Even though we hope our plan works and the golem will be able to steal the cloak for us, we must be prepared for the worst. I will not be on the battlefield with you but will provide as much protection as I can to our army."

Merlin saw the fear in the council's eyes as they heard his last words. "Do not be fearful, I will be following Brianna's golem. If Stygian sees through our masquerade, I will be able to act quickly. I have supplied all of the men with enchanted armor. They must still be skillful in combat, but will have an added layer of protection from mortal wounds. We also have Echo and his fae. Their special talents as fast-flying fae will allow us to manuever quickly and have multiple vantage points to access the battle."

The council was still uneasy but trusted Merlin. As Merlin finished speaking, Cameron came in with Brianna's golem.

Everyone in the room was mesmerized by her beauty and intrigued by her existence. Merlin turned his attention to the golem. "Young maiden, do you know what your mission is?"

The golem nodded her understanding to Merlin. She then began to speak. "I am to locate the one named Stygian and offer myself as his wife to save my love. Once I am able to win Stygian's trust, I will steal his cloak and drink the elixir Merlin has prepared for me to transport me back to the keep."

"Very good, my child, you have remembered well." Merlin breathed a sigh of relief. Another crack of thunder rang through the keep. This time it was closer and the lightning illuminated the sky. A slight drizzle turned into torrential rain. The sentries could barely see in front of them. The scouts could barely retain their posts as they watched over the Kelpie Ring. The sky grew darker and only the lightning would illuminate the darkness.

Brianna's golem was sent out to meet Stygian at the Ring. She ran as if the devil himself was upon her heels. Her lungs felt like exploding, each breath more difficult than the last. She had to arrive at the Ring before Stygian. The sentries and scouts watched the beautiful fae run through the treacherous terrain occasionally slipping and scrambling back up. She was their one and only hope. The golem finally made it to the Ring. A flash of lightning followed by a horrific crack illuminated the Ring. As she peered into its depths, the golem could see Stygian astride a menacing horse trailed by a large army. The horse's nostrils flared and its red eyes pierced her soul. Another strike of lightning hit closer this time and the golem could see Stygian reaching through the portal toward her.

Stygian could not believe his luck when he saw Brianna on the other side of the Ring. "What a foolish child she is to believe she is able to stop me," he laughed maniacally. She was an alluring creature. Standing in the rain she was soaked to the bone. Her gown barely left anything to the imagination as it clung to her supple body. Stygian lost himself for a moment before realizing she was a temptress and needed to be punished for her disobedience. He began to reach through the portal, but the barrier still resisted his entry. Using the combined powers of the shire horses and his army, Stygian created an electric pulse to obliterate the barrier. The pulse created a blinding light along with a blast that threw the golem several feet into the forest. The storm was no more and darkness overtook the land. Stygian and his army now stood in the realm of men.

CHAPTER 18

Fury and Chaos

STYGIAN WAS FILLED with unbridled rage and excitement. "Finally, my time has come." The barrier was destroyed and his army was in the mortal realm. "Now to see my future bride." Stygian walked toward the unconscious fae. The blast from the breach had thrown her several feet away from the Ring. She lay motionless on the forest floor. Stygian's carnal urges were difficult to contain. Before he could take her, he needed to defeat the fae village and Asheboro keep. She would be his whether she agreed to it or not. The Ailey bloodline would be tied to his. Taking a moment to caress her cheek and allow his hands to wander down her slender neck, he could not stop himself from wandering further down her body to her supple breasts.

The golem, thought to be Brianna by Stygian, began to slowly rouse from her injury. Her head was throbbing and her body stiff. Even though she was made of clay, she could still feel as a human would; she could feel hands upon her body but could not stop them. Her eyes began to flutter awake. Once they were able to focus in the darkness, she screamed in horror as she saw a grotesque, malformed creature hunched over her. Its hands wandering over her body as if she belonged to it. "My sweet, what a welcome you provide your future husband," he said as he caressed her cheek. "I have come to save my village," the golem stated.

"I know my spell was broken, Brianna. Cameron is alive and well. The small inkling I had to spare your love was obliterated the moment you escaped my prison." Brianna began to shake and fear was rising within her. "You, my dear, will now become my wife and watch all that you hold dear die. If you wish to save a few souls as servants, I will grant you that mercy. Know this, once I become King of both realms, you will have my children, your sisters will become my concubines, and your brothers will become my personal slaves. Your parents will surely die."

"What kind words from a gentleman. A proposal that includes death and mayhem. How can a girl refuse? I was offering myself to save my village, but I will kill myself before I allow you anywhere near me. If you wish to have all the power of both realms, you first must find Merlin."

Stygian faltered for a moment when he heard the name of the ancient fae. "What did you say, girl?"

"Merlin holds the key. Without him, you will never be able to truly rule. He will be your nemesis until the end of time." Brianna gave him a confident smirk and watched as his face contorted with the new information Brianna parted on him. "Now, if you wish to broker a deal, I can perhaps help you locate him in exchange for the lives of my family and village. The mortals, if they must perish, then so be it." Stygian could not believe what he was hearing. Merlin was alive! How could that be? Merlin left Solasta over 50 years ago, and the Ailey family thought him dead. But Brianna must be telling the truth.

She stood her ground and looked at the maniacal demon in front of her. "The once-sweet Brianna has now changed her view on the mortals. "You are willing to allow them to be brought to the slaughter for your village and family to be spared?" Brianna nodded in agreement. The wheels in Stygian's head began to turn. The most hideous grin began to appear on his face. "My dear, there is no deal. I believe you are willing to make any deal that could save your family and village. What I am asking is that you willingly give yourself to me and bear my heir. Perhaps I would consider saving your family and the treacherous fae who turned their backs on me."

Brianna's eyes grew wide and filled with horror. This hideous monstrosity wanted to bed her and then have her bear his child! She did not know how to even respond. The idea of his pus-filled hands touching her made her skin crawl. How could she ever allow him to take her willingly? "I cannot give myself to you. I belong to Laird Cedar-Kellen. He is my one true love. I will not concede my virtue to your grotesque machinations."

Stygian knew this would be her reply. "Then I guess we are at an impasse, my dear. If you are not willing to give yourself freely to me, then I will take what I want." Stygian signaled one of his minions to grab Brianna and ordered them to take her back to his castle in Solasta.

"Make sure our honored guest has no way of escaping. Place her in the dungeons and shackle her with silver." Two dark fae grabbed Brianna. She attempted to fight her attackers but her efforts were futile. Stygian ordered the fae to march on as Brianna's screams for help fell on deaf ears. The dark army led by Stygian continued their path of destruction. Trees were ablaze as large boulders began to roll through the path toward Asheboro keep. The ominous sky began to roar once again with thunder and lightning. Stygian could now command the elements. His powers grew stronger as he drained the Kelpie Ring of its magical essence.

The army marched on to Asheboro Keep. Stygian never noticed the hidden figure in the woods watching the army's every move. If he had only taken the time to analyze his surroundings, he would have found what he was seeking within an arm's length.

King Arthur and his men were prepared for the battle to come. They were not prepared for the onslaught of debris that began pelting them. Ronan and Echo combined their powers in an attempt to deflect the debris, but Stygian's magic was too strong' The villagers watched as the beautiful forest was engulfed with flames. The Ailey sisters peered from their chamber window wishing they could join the fight to fend off the impending destruction. They prayed to the elders that their families would remain safe within the keep walls. Once luscious vineyards and groves were quickly replaced by ash as the consuming fire spread like water spilled from a fallen pitcher. Laird Asheboro quickly gathered his men and the fae. Merlin gave specific instructions as to what each group must do to ensure their victory. The knights and village men were to be set as the sentries, while the fae would be hidden within the battlements, led by River and Rune. The dark king would be seeking the fae first to destroy them so that the mortals would lose any advantage possible. The fae enchanted the weapons and strengthened the protective border Merlin had placed around the keep. The warriors stood looking out from the turrets watching the destruction coming closer to them. They stood brave and unflinching with weapons at the ready.

The horizon grew darker until the day became night and the inky black sky consumed any light that attempted to shine. Stygian's army now crested the final hill before reaching Haven Village. Stygian and his black shire horses created shockwaves through the earth, tumbling the village structures as if they were children's toys. Everything the fae had worked for, cultivated, and built within seconds was destroyed. Jada and her daughters looked out the western window from Brianna's chamber. Their eyes filled with horror and tears. Their once-enchanting and bustling village lay in ruins.

Stygian could be seen leading the small but mighty army with his demonic shire horses in the forefront. Aurora and Celeste were shaking with anger. While the men were out protecting the keep, they were locked away. "We must do something," Celeste said in frustration. Jada looked at her eldest and gently placed her hand over her daughter's. "Celeste, we must wait for the signal from Merlin."

Celeste looked at her mother strangely.

"What do you mean we must wait for Merlin's signal?" Aurora chimed in.

"Before Merlin left us, he spoke to me. Not knowing how Stygian was able to cloak his thoughts, Merlin did not want Stygian to be able to read ours. To elude this enchantment, Merlin only provided a small piece of the grand plan to each of us. Celeste you will use your powers to blind the army and then show them the way back to the Kelpie Ring. Aurora, you will enchant the earth to feel as if they are walking on molten lava constantly changing and chasing them. Merlin has cloaked himself near the Kelpie Ring."

The women looked awestruck. Merlin had truly thought of everything. He knew the golem would fail and Stygian would cross into the mortal realm. He would use the sisters to drive back the army and lead them into Solasta. The battle that is to come would only last long enough for Merlin to enter Solasta and begin to repair the barrier between the worlds. He would use blood magic to seal the enchantment, allowing anyone to pass through the barrier. Only Stygian would not be able to come and go as he pleased.

The enchantment would be made to specifically keep him out. "But mother, this still does not solve our problem. Yes, Stygian will be banished once again to Solasta but there will always be the chance of his return."

"My dear Celeste," Jada stroked her cheek. "Merlin has solved this problem as well. The golem we have sent has been poisoned. She was never meant to retrieve the cloak. The moment Stygian takes the golem for himself, she will begin to fuse to his skin and immobilize him. As her flesh melts and sticks to him, the toxins mixed into her clay will begin to seep from her and enter his body. It will be a slow and painful death."

Guinevere then spoke. "What of the cloak and Brianna?"

Jada shook her head. "This I do not know. Merlin told me to trust him and that my dear Brianna will awaken safely."

As Jada finished explaining to the women what was to pass, the first blows of battle arrived. The Keep shook with a ferocity they had never felt before. The enchantment worked well. The barrier held, and no damage came to the keep. The sentries prepared their arrows and catapults. Fires were lit and the oil boiled above the portcullis to ensure whoever dared pass through the gates would be immediately incinerated. Stygian and his army began their barrage of attacks; the shire horses continuously sent shock waves, making it difficult for the men to stand their ground. The shield was holding, but cracks were beginning to emerge. The sentries were true to their marks but the dark fae would not fall. "Hurry, men!" shouted the captain of the sentries. He continued to shout out orders. "Prepare the catapults!"

The knights began to grow impatient with the fae and wanted to charge Stygian and his dark army. Sir Galahad reminded his men of Merlin's warning. "If we breach the barrier first, our protective charms will no longer be. Stygian would be able to easily snap his fingers and kill us all in one motion." They had to stand their ground and wait for Stygian to come to them. The fae who were hidden in the battlements began to deploy their magic. Roots and vines rose from the ground to entangle the army, creating a wall of thorns to halt their momentum. Stygian let out a maniacal laugh. "This is child's play. How did Maximus ever fool me? Roots and vines are no match for my powers."

Stygian obliterated the thorn wall with a simple wave of his hand, allowing the dark army to continue to march forward. Cameron was growing anxious as the enemy continued its march toward the keep. He had to keep to Merlin's plan. He was not to show himself until he could see the whites of Stygian's eyes. Merlin told him the simple sight of him would enrage Stygian to the point of madness.

Even though Stygian would believe he had captured Brianna, the fact still remained that Cameron was alive, had escaped his curse, and would always attempt to save Brianna. The rage would blind Stygian, assuring he would falter in battle. Cameron needed to see Brianna one more time before the battle took over their thoughts. He raced from his post to the chamber. He fumbled with the keys as he attempted to gain entry.

"Quickly, girls! Stand behind me," yelled Jada, poised to attack whoever was coming. Cameron burst into the room, and Guinevere nearly pelted him with a chair. "It's me! Cameron!" he shouted. The women quickly softened their stance and nearly collapsed from their fright.

"I wish for one last moment with Brianna. This may be my last opportunity. I want her to know how much she means to me. I will go to the ends of the Earth to save her, even if that may mean I no longer draw breath."

Guinevere understood how important this last moment meant to the Laird. "Jada, let us give the young couple a few moments to themselves."

"Thank you, my Queen. Jada, would this be suitable for you?" asked Cameron. Jada nodded her acceptance.

"Thank you, milady." Cameron walked over to Brianna's bedside and pulled up a chair. Gently he lifted her hand and placed a kiss upon it. She was an angelic beauty in a deep sleep. How he wished she would open her eyes and bless him with her radiant smile.

"My dove, I wish we could have had this conversation in better circumstances.Know that I go into battle for you, for our future, and for our families. I promise you when this battle is over, I will be waiting with bated breath for your beautiful violet eyes to flutter open. My Brianna, I love you beyond the stars and the moon; may our fates bring us together once again."

He stood and placed a kiss on Brianna's forehead. He looked at her peaceful sleep, knowing how much she sacrificed for the possibility of them being together one day. Before he left the ladies to return to battle, he walked over to the small writing desk and quickly penned a note to his future bride. Once he'd placed his thoughts onto paper, he sealed it and walked to the solar to meet once again with the Queen and Ailey women.

"Thank you for these few moments. If for any reason I do not return from this battle, please give Brianna this letter. I love her beyond all measure. I want her to know that she is my one and only. Even if I depart this Earth before she wakes, my heart and allegiance will always be with her." Cameron handed Jada the letter and gave his final bow to the ladies before returning to the war that awaited him. He slowly left their chamber locking the women once again in their rooms. As he returned to his post, he asked his most-trusted guard, Liam, to watch over the women and stand at their door to assure their safety. "Liam, you must promise me to guard our Queen and my future bride. Do not leave your post no matter what may happen."

"With every fiber in my being, Laird Cedar-Kellen. No harm will come to the women." Liam shook Cameron's hand before he left for his new post.

Cameron returned to his post with Laird Asheboro to continue their watch, releasing the fae and sentries as Merlin had directed them to. They were losing by the looks of things. River and Rune were leading the fae. River dodged every boulder that came his way as he directed from the sky the regiments. Rune with his Herculean strength helped to load the catapults and move them into position. The barrier had weakened enough to allow blazing boulders to enter the keep, destroying the inner bailey. Soon the barrier would be no more and the full force of Stygian's powers would be unleashed. The village men began to fall prey to the onslaught. Arthur's knights waited in anticipation to join in the fight. The keep would not hold for much longer.

Stygian was not a fool; he knew the keep was protected. It was only a matter of time before the spell would release with his barrage of powers. He then would be able to sit back and unleash hell upon all his enemies.

Merlin watched as the dark army made its way to the keep. Once Stygian was out of his sight, he began to repair the Kelpie Ring. Stygian was too consumed by the impending battle to notice the magic occurring at the Ring. The once beautiful ornate bridge had been obliterated with Stygian's entry. Merlin began to weave the Ring back together. Each gem that was strewn throughout the forest slowly emerged from the rubble. Merlin then began his incantation as he cut his hand.

"Runes near and far join us on this day of judgment. Darkness has come to the mortal realm and with it, its King. Help us ancient fae to return to our once beautiful lands, destroy the darkness that has arrived, and summon it to your deepest hell. As each stone is placed on your Ring seal them with your power. I, Merlin, the seventh son of the seventh son, summon the power of the ancient families to banish the dark fae Stygian from the mortal realm."

As Merlin spoke his last words, the gemstones aligned and launched themselves onto the remnants of the once-standing bridge. The stones moved back into place, creating a beautiful arch with a reflecting waterfall and pool. The gems vibrated with power and seemed as if they were living beings. Assuring that he was not seen, Merlin slowly made his way to the Kelpie Ring. With his wounded hand he gently placed a drop of his blood around the crystal-clear pond. Entering the waters, he began to repeat his enchantment. As he spoke the words, he placed his hands in the water to wash away the cut he had created. It was time. The Ring was restored. The magic in place. For Stygian there was only one way into Solasta, and he would never be able to return.

He needed to signal Jada for her daughters to begin the next part of his plan. Once Merlin entered Solasta, he would not return to the mortal realm until Stygian was in his grave. Merlin had given an amulet to Jada before he left the keep. The amulet was linked to his. Closing his eyes, Merlin held the amulet tight until it began to glow and pulse with life. As the amulet grew brighter, Merlin could sense Stygian's power and thoughts. Somehow they would become linked. He had to work quickly before Stygian realized what was to come. Jada felt her pocket begin to vibrate. She immediately pulled the amulet out and saw that it was emanating an immense light. This was the sign. They had to work quickly before more of their men were lost to Stygian's army.

CHAPTER 19

Destruction

MERLIN KNEW THERE would be many casualties in this war. He worked as quickly as he could in hopes of saving the villagers and Asheboro Keep. He sent his signal to Jada using their shared amulets. Once the women began their enchantments and he entered Solasta, he would send a spark into the air to signal Laird Asheboro and the King. Now he had to return to the place he once called home. He should have no issues, as the dark fae were with Stygian, except for the two who captured the golem. As Merlin entered Solasta, the barrier protection finally broke over the keep. The dark army rejoiced with their sudden luck. Sir Galahad and his knights were at the ready, Cameron only paces behind them. "Tell me when this murderous villain is near!" Cameron yelled to the knights.

The dark army was within the archers' reach. The catapults began to unleash their power with balls of fire toward the enemy. The first wave of men rushed the dark army. Swords and spears clashed and clanged as the men collided. Boulders ablaze fell near the men on the field, landing their marks. Stygian held back, wanting the mortal army to feel they had the upper hand. He watched as men and fae began to fall. He glided his hand in front of him, deflecting every single arrow and boulder. With a simple flick of his fingers, the arrows and boulders flew back to the keep, killing a third of the sentinels.

Cameron became enraged. Not being able to contain himself, he charged the dark fae with his eyes focused on his target, Stygian. Cameron trusted his weapons. His shield and sword were enchanted by Merlin. Every blow landed its mark. Stygian laughed with delight as he saw the Laird begin to charge in his direction. No matter how many dark fae fell, they would return to life. "What dark magic is this?" yelled Sir Percival. Arthur's knights were valiant. As they stood by the village men, a calm washed over them as the dark fae began to retreat. They were beginning to take ground. As they moved forward, they did not realize the fae they had just slain behind them began to rise again. The dark army was small but could not be killed.

Stygian laughed as he saw the terror begin to move through the villagers' army. His army would never fall unless he were to be injured. He watched as the knight's futile efforts began to slow. The mortal army was becoming weary. Stygian's army was regaining the field advantage.

The dark fae began to slash, thrust, and plunge their weapons into the men.

Even though the villagers' armor was enchanted, they still could not deflect every move. Laird Asheboro and King

Arthur looked upon the battle in horror. They were losing, and the dark army was beginning to breach the portcullis. "When will Merlin signal us? Our men are being slaughtered!" yelled Laird Asheboro to King Arthur.

"Trust in Merlin, he has never let me down. He brought me to Excalibur and through every battle. He has never faltered," Arthur reassured him.

The men continued to look on as their army was quickly diminishing. The Ailey brothers rushed to the front of the battle. River combined their rings and hoped it was enough magic to pause the immortal fae long enough for the villagers to retreat. As the rings merged and the brothers joined hands, a blinding light emerged. River yelled to Ronan, "Now!" A lightning bolt shot through the heavens and landed feet from the villagers, creating such force the dark fae were flung back into the forest. Arrows and catapults continued to fly, but to no avail. In the distance, a burst of light flew through the air. "There it is," cried Arthur. We may enter the battle!" Both men ran down the battlements toward the portcullis, ready to defend the keep as the dark fae breached the front gates. The boiling oil and tar did nothing to the fae. Their features grew more grotesque as the tar and oil melted their skin, clinging to their extremities. Arthur and Laird Asheboro took a steadying breath before they began to rail against the intruders.

In Brianna's chamber, Celeste began her illusion. First she must blind the dark fae. Once that was achieved she then was to create the illusion of reversing the direction of the fae. Aurora waited for Celeste's signal. The dark army did not know what was happening. One moment they were breaching the keep's portcullis, and the next they could not see anything. They froze for a moment, allowing the village army to push them back. The dark fae were now outside the gates, clutching at their eyes. Stygian did not understand why his men were now outside of the keep.

Celeste continued the enchantment, guiding the dark army back toward the kelpie Ring. "Now!" yelled Celeste. Aurora then began to convert the earth into molten lava. The knights and village army instantly ran back into the keep to avoid the fatal river of flowing lava. There now was a divide between both armies. As the dark army continued to battle their imaginary foes, the keep began to reinforce their positions. Both Celeste and Aurora worked in tandem to push the dark army back toward the Ring. Stygian was seething with rage as he saw his army acting like fools, battling thin air. He did not know what was causing this change of events.

As he continued to observe the battle, Stygian realized there was a growing river of molten lava following his men, blocking them from the keep. They attempted to walk through the lava, becoming stuck in place as it cooled. "It must be the Ailey sisters," he thought to himself. He attempted to stop the lava flow, but his magic did not work. How was this possible? His magic had never failed him. Once again, he attempted to stop the flow of lava but it continued.

Even though his men could not be killed, they would not last much longer if continuously being set upon by the molten earth. Stygian could not go into battle, or he would risk being injured and breaking the spell that allowed his dark army to be immortal. He had to stop the Ailey sisters somehow. They were the ones thwarting his progress, he was sure of it. Celeste and Aurora continued in their enchantments. Jada placed a hand on each of her daughters to supply them with more magic to continue their fight. "Celeste and Aurora, I love you! As my hands touch yours may my powers amplify yours."

They were gaining ground and pushing the dark army further and further away from the keep. The dark army began to run in the opposite direction of the keep. "You fools! What are you about? The keep is not toward me." The weary army could not continue. Even though they were immortal, it did not mean that they had an unlimited supply of energy. They could no longer hold up their swords and shields. Unknown to Stygian was that the illusion Celeste had created caused the dark army to envision an ancient dragon of times past. It pursued, them blowing incinerating flames. The dark fae knew of the legendary dragons and of their all-consuming powers. They would never survive an attack from such a noble beast. Dragons were known to judge the hearts of men. If they found your heart wanting, you would be instantly consumed, your soul forever banished to the depths of hell.

The army no longer listened to Stygian. They ran as swiftly as they could, causing Stygian to be knocked from his horse. His legs became tangled in the reins of his steed, Abyss. The crush of dark fae running toward the Kelpie Ring forced the horse to buck and turn back to follow them. Stygian was trampled. Instantly, the enchantment was broken and his men began to fall. The molten lava continued to creep toward the group, enveloping any of the fallen or injured fae. Horror began to take over Stygian's emotions. He was injured, the enchantment had been broken, and now he was being dragged back into Solasta.

The cloak Stygian wore was beginning to tear and the crystals were lost. He could feel the magic within him weakening. Attempting to save himself and the cloak, Stygian summoned the earth elements to create a wall between himself and the consuming lava. It would only hold for a short time, but it would be enough for him to gain his wits. The pain was insurmountable; he knew there were several bones broken. Once the wall of earth was in place, Stygian moved his concentration to his body. He was not able to heal himself, but he had the ability to float above his men.

As he rose, Stygian saw the carnage that was left behind by both his and the mortal army. It was inconceivable. "How am I losing?" He had underestimated the Ailey family and King Arthur with his knights. His army was defeated, the remaining survivors driven back into Solasta. He needed to regroup and form a new plan. He could not summon much more magic due to his injuries, coupled with the loss of several amulets. He had just enough energy for one final blow. Being above the stampeding fae and lava, he was able to see the keep with the villagers surrounding the front gates. Cameron and Arthur's knights were front and center.

A menacing grin grew on his face as he placed his bloody hands together. Concentrating all his power, Stygian created a massive ball of fire. It was so fierce even Stygian could not protect himself from its enveloping inferno. If he could aim it just right, it would land in the molten lava in front of the men creating an explosion. "This will allow me to escape and kill Brianna's one true love. It's a pity I will not be able to see the results of my efforts." The ball grew larger and larger, Stygian's hands were becoming blistered, the stench of burning flesh enveloped his nostrils. His skin was beginning to sag and melt away. Once Stygian could not endure the pain any longer, he let the fire ball loose.

It flew through the air, incinerating everything in its path toward the keep. Within moments, the released fireball landed feet from the men. The impact came with such force the earth shook, toppling the men that were running from the explosive spell. Cameron had seen the massive ball of flame being hurdled toward the keep. He had quickly sounded the retreat to attempt to save as many of the men as possible. He was the last to retreat. He hoped beyond all hope that the enchanted armor Merlin provided him would keep him from death. As the molten lava splashed from the impact, all Cameron could do was shield himself among the dead and place his escutcheon over his head. The heat was unbearable. Cameron attempted to stay conscious, but his senses were overwhelmed. The stench of the bodies burning and the immense heat emanating from the lava flows were too powerful to withstand.

He had to continue moving, but he did not know how. If the lava did not cease, soon he would be completely consumed. Attempting to move further away from the lava, Cameron began climbing over the bodies that lead him to the keep. The smoke and the smell of burning flesh was too much for Cameron to endure. The last vision Cameron was able to see before falling unconscious was Arthur and his knights running toward him, attempting to reach him before he was overtaken.

CHAPTER 20

Revelations

CELESTE AND AURORA fell to their knees with the aftershocks from Stygian's blast. Their enchantment was broken the moment they lost their concentration. The lava instantly disappeared; the earth was no longer rubble. Once the enchantment was lifted, all that was left were the unfortunate souls that did not survive Stygian's onslaught. The dark fae who had remained, instantly died the moment Stygian became injured. Arthur and his men stood in shock at the sea of bodies. Laird Asheboro and King Arthur rushed toward Cameron. They could not believe he had survived the blast. Merlin's armor truly saved him. His skin was badly burned, but he was still alive. Arthur's knights surrounded Cameron and lifted the fallen Laird.

Cameron was first brought into the kitchens to be stripped of his armor and clothing. They ordered a cool bath for him to soothe his skin. No one had Merlin's magic to ease the pain, but they did have the Ailey sisters and their mother. Maximus went to the chamber where the ladies awaited their release. He summoned the girls and Jada to assist the injured Laird. Guinevere remained to watch over the sleeping Brianna. Carrying Brianna's poultices and salves, Jada followed her husband to the injured Laird. When she first laid eyes on Cameron she let out a gasp of horror before collecting herself. She began ordering the knights. "I need strips of linen to cover his wounds, a cool bath to stop the burning. Sir Galahad please add this rose water to the cooling bath and dip all the linens within its waters. Sir Percival, the basket— remove the salve with the leather cloth bound around it. Sir Gawain, gather as much moss as possible. We will not have enough to cover his body."

As quickly as Jada gave the demands, the knights dispersed and returned with the needed items. Jada first created a tea using the milk of the poppy to allow Cameron rest and not feel the soon-to-come bath. To ensure no infection would take over his body, the knights lowered the Laird into the rose bath. Jada gently sponged lavender oil over his body as she bathed, him removing all the impurities she could find. Cameron groaned with each touch. "I know, Laird Cedar-Kellen, it is painful but necessary." Cameron even with the milk of the poppy was in and out of consciousness.

Once Jada was satisfied with Cameron's bath, the men lifted him out of the tub and placed him on the table. Jada and her daughters began to quickly lather Cameron with the honey, lavender, rose, and poppy salve to soothe Cameron's skin. They hoped he would have minimal scarring from his burns. "If only Brianna was awake, she would have been able to heal him. His body would have renewed without a single mar left," lamented Jada. He was truly blessed; his skin was blistered from the heat but only his hands were the most damaged. The poultices and salves would heal the blisters, but his hands would need to be cared for tenderly. If Brianna awoke within a week, he would be able to regain the movement in his hands.

The women worked quickly. Within the hour, the Laird was bathed, covered in bandages, and placed in the bedchamber next to Brianna's room. All they could do now was pray to the gods that Cameron would recover from his wounds and Brianna would awaken in time to save his hands.

Solasta

As soon as he had unleashed his fireball, Stygian was thrown back into the Kelpie Ring. Stunned, he did not wake for a few moments. He was disoriented and did not realize he was in Solasta. His hands were gruesome. Pieces of flesh clung by mere threads with blisters forming upon other blisters. Careful not to use his them, Stygian attempted to rise, but his leg was broken from the stampede. Using the limited magic he had left, he attempted to float toward the entrance of Solasta. When this failed, he called for anyone to assist him.

"My King, how may I be of service?" It was one of his minions who had retreated in the first wave. "Help me to the entrance of Solasta." The duo worked in tandem to drag

Stygian towards the portal. He could feel something was different, the magic was altered. Slowly raising his hand, he pressed into the Kelpie Ring expecting for it to disappear into the mortal realm.

The instant his hand touched the Ring he was flung back with such force he and the dark fae were knocked backward. Another of his minions came to his master and assisted him. "What has happened to the Ring?" Stygian asked the minion.

"I do not know, sire; a few of our dark army attempted to go through the Ring before you came through. They were instantly incinerated. Someone has tampered with the magic and now we are locked into the fae realm."

Stygian released a guttural roar in frustration. He had underestimated the Ailey family. Now he knew what Brianna had said was true. Merlin was alive and aiding the mortals. The only satisfaction he gained for the day's events was the fact that he had Brianna. Soon her family would return to save her. He had to prepare for their arrival. Stygian and his minions made their way back to his castle. His injuries were beginning to fester, and he needed a healer. Stygian smirked at the thought of Brianna touching him with gentle caresses and bandaging his wounds. The fae was mad to think she would be a willing participant in his healing, but his delusions consumed his every thought. Even though he had lost the battle, Stygian believed he would still conquer the mortal realm. He simply needed time.

Brianna's golem sat in a dark and damp dungeon. The rats were her only companions as they scurried past her feet. She was cold and sore from the hard stones she laid upon. The evil minions did not even have the courtesy to allow her a small pallet to lie on, solely a bucket to use as her privy. "I suppose I should be grateful for the small plate with molded cheese and bread." Her words echoed within the empty chamber, followed by a deafening silence. Suddenly in the shadows, the golem caught a figure moving toward her. Frightened that it was Stygian coming for her, she attempted to hide herself in the darkest corner of her cell.

The object came closer. A soft voice beckoned to her. "Child, are you all right?"

The golem slowly lifted her head to peer at the cell door. To her astonishment there stood Merlin. She did not want to show her excitement and alert her captors. "You made it into Solasta!" the golem spoke.

"Yes, my dear. I do not have much time before Stygian arrives. He has been badly injured requiring healing. He will come to you for restoration. He does not know you have no power to do so. Try your best to tempt him into your cell. I will disguise myself within the dungeon waiting for him to enter. Once he is in your cell, assure his back is to the door. Remember you must take your elixir to activate the toxins within your skin and spell.

"The moment you and Stygian touch, your body will begin to merge with his to allow for the toxins within you to enter him. I will remove his cloak and all his magic." Brianna's golem looked at Merlin with a sad understanding. Her life was short and soon it would be gone to return to the earth it was molded from.

"I understand Merlin." slowly the golem reached into her gown pocket and removed the hidden vial of poison. "To Brianna and Cameron, may they have everlasting love." The golem lifted the small bottle to her lips and drank the activating solution.

It broke his heart to see such a beautiful and kind creature being destroyed. He wanted to provide her some solace but did not know how. She was made to kill Stygian and allow Merlin an opportunity to reclaim the cloak of enchanted crystals. "I will be with you, little one, do not fear. Your sacrifice will be rewarded in heaven by the gods." As Merlin placed a rose in the golem's hand, a commotion broke the silence within the dungeon. Merlin hurried to obscure himself from sight. Stygian and his minions stormed the dungeon, searching for Brianna.

"My bride, your future husband, is in need of your gifts. Come to your cell door and restore my injuries."

Brianna's golem fumed with anger; how dare he summon her for a restorative. "You should have plenty of assistance with your minions surrounding you. How dare you ask me to heal you when I have been treated with so little respect and honor. May you succumb to your injuries and suffer in Hell for all eternity."

Stygian laughed at her retort. "Listen to me, you obstinate child! You will heal me and become my bride. If you dare to defy me you will live to regret it."

Brianna stood in her cell, crossed her arms, and gave Stygian a devilish smirk. "I …Dare… to …. Defy…. You." Stygian roared with anger. He did not have much magic left after the battle but had enough to blast open the cell door. At that same moment Merlin used the sound of the blast to stun Stygian's lackeys, leaving only himself, the golem, and Stygian standing in the room. Stygian stormed into Brianna's cell, lifting her into the air. "You will do as I say, whore! I am done with your games." Stygian attempted to throw Brianna to the ground, but he was not able to release his grip. Her skin was beginning to meld to his. His hands were so burnt he could not feel the toxins entering his body. The golem began to laugh while horror overtook Stygian.

Merlin emerged from the shadows. He walked up to the pair in the cell. "Well done, my dove. Place your hands on Stygian's face and do not let go." The golem did as she was commanded. Merlin began to cut away at the crystal cloak. It was tattered with numerous crystals lost during the battle. There was still just enough magic left in the cloak to allow Merlin to seal Solasta and escape into the mortal realm. Stygian struggled and fought to let Brianna go, but it was useless. The golem held tightly onto the Dark Fae King, allowing her hands to merge with his face. Merlin was deft in his efforts to remove the cloak. Once he had collected all the items he needed, Merlin looked at the distorted couple slowly melting into each other.

"My dove, now wrap your legs around the dark king." The golem did as was requested.

"What magic is this, Merlin!"

"For one who is all knowing and powerful, did you not know of golems and how they are created?" Merlin answered with a sly smile. "You were so enamored and crazed you did not think of the old ways, Stygian. Have you forgotten so quickly the methods you used on Braun? Brianna's golem was a bit more refined, of course. She was made just for you. The earth that she was created from contained flowers from the Elders. Perhaps you may know of them; foxglove, hemlock, oleander, and my favorite, lily of the valley. They were carefully woven into her design. We knew you would not be able to control yourself and eventually touch or take her unwillingly. I just did not expect it to be so quickly. Your death will be slow as she continues to melt into your body. The hemlock will soon paralyze your body but keep you awake long enough to see all that you hold dear become dust."

Merlin stepped out of the cell and watched as Stygian's body became paralyzed and contorted by the lethal poisons he absorbed. He released the golem's consciousness to allow it to die peacefully. Merlin did not want to leave anything to chance; he was confident Stygian would die a slow and painful death but something still unsettled him.

Merlin used the cell as a tomb for Stygian. Brick by brick Merlin magically placed them around the couple, still embraced in their deathly struggle.

He guaranteed there would be no way out of the coffin he had created for his mortal enemy. Once the first layer of bricks was placed, he allowed for a singular opening to remain as he assembled Stygian's minions into a pile of fae carcasses. They would burn for their betrayal of the Solastian fae. Merlin searched the dungeon for any material that would burn and ignite the fallen fae. As he searched each cell, there was one that was bolted and sealed by powerful magic. The door to the cell had a small opening to supply food but nothing more.

Merlin released the spell then carefully opened the door. The chamber was dark, and there was no movement. Merlin wondered why they would have bolted and magically sealed a chamber if there was no one inside. Merlin was not foolish enough to walk into a dark room. He grabbed a torch from the outside wall and slowly peered in. To his surprise there was a fae crumpled in the corner of the cell. He could not make out if it was a male or female fae for they were emaciated and past recognition. Whoever the fae was, Merlin could sense their power. Stygian must not have been able to strip it from the fae.

In an instant, the fae was on its feet running toward Merlin, screaming like a madman. He dropped the torch and the room became engulfed with flames. Merlin acted quickly and stunned the fairy in mid-air. The fairy crashed to the floor. He knew the fae only wanted to be freed from its prison. Knowing the fae was immobile, he carefully approached to view the fae's face. To his astonishment it was Magnus! How did he not know? Why did Maximus not mention their brother was imprisoned?

Tears began to fall down Merlin's cheeks as he saw the state of his brother. It had been over 50 years since he had left his home. His brothers had been healthy and strong with young families. "How did this come to pass?" Merlin, forgetting the flames created by the torch, rushed to pull his brother away from the consuming inferno. He placed his brother by the stairs exiting the dungeon. Needing to finish what he started, Merlin gathered all of the dark fae into one cell and locked them inside. He set them ablaze. He then turned to Stygian who was entombed in the next cell.

He placed a second set of bricks over the coffin before completely sealing Stygian into his final resting place. He left him a small candle to illuminate the dark tomb. "May you never see the light of day again." Stygian could no longer speak. All he could do was stare into Merlin's cold icy blue eyes. The golem was no longer visible. It would take some time for Brianna to awaken. Once the spell has completely dissipated, she would be able to provide aid to any of the fallen men who were able to survive the onslaught of battle. The fire was beginning to grow. Merlin needed to leave the dungeon. Grabbing the cloak, he was able to cocoon his brother within it and magically lift him through the stairs. It seemed an eternity for Merlin as he navigated the dark winding halls of the castle with his brother in tow.

Reaching the throne room, Merlin felt safe enough to pause and heal his brother. He gently placed his hand on

Magnus's head. A slow light began to emerge, illuminating the barely alive fae. Color was returning to his cheeks. His body, once cold, began to warm. Magnus' eyes slowly began to flutter open. Terror raked his body as he saw a figure leaning over him. They were saying something to him but he could not make out the words. His senses were not yet fully functioning. They did not harm him. It seemed that they wanted to wipe away the grime from his face.

Suddenly his head was being lifted and a goblet placed to his mouth. He did not want to drink, as he was afraid the liquid was poisoned. Merlin realized his brother did not recognize him nor understand that he was there to help. Concentrating on his brother, Merlin projected his thoughts to him. "Magnus, it is me, Merlin. I am here to help you. Drink from the goblet." His brothers' body began to relax. He once again attempted to bring water to his brothers' lips. This time he drank. The goblet was quickly drained. Magnus raised his hand, placing it on Merlin's cheek. With a raspy voice, he said, "Merlin." He was finally able to rest. Magnus took a steadying breath and fell unconscious in Merlin's arms.

CHAPTER 21

Solasta

THE DARK KING had finally been defeated. His castle was engulfed in flames after Merlin left, assuring all who remained inside would perish. There were a few pockets of traitorous fae left in Solasta, but they were quickly dispatched. Merlin worked tirelessly to hunt them down, extinguishing their flames. The destruction Stygian left behind astounded Merlin. Each village he encountered was a shell of its former glory. Buildings were reduced to rubble, the wells bubbled with a black toxic sludge, and the once-beautiful meadows and forests were decaying heaps of wood filled with maggots. His once-glorious and prosperous home was no longer alive.

The only village left standing was his familial home of Luminia. He was able to transport Magnus to one of the few homes left standing. Magnus' recovery would be an arduous process, but he was determined to save his brother. He would need Brianna's healing powers to assure his full recovery. Before he could leave Solasta, he had to begin the healing process of the land. He would then be able to return to the mortal realm and have Brianna assist with Magnus.

Solasta was now quiet, no buzz of the bees or babbling of the brooks. The land was poisoned by the darkness. Merlin was able to remove all the crystals from the grotesque cloak Stygian once owned. He examined each and every one. They varied in their magical power. Unfortunately, the magic could not be restored to its former owners, as they had long been deceased. He could funnel the magic back into the land to see if he could restore Solasta. He first began with the water sources around the realm. Merlin would place a crystal in a stream, watching as the darkness would be pulled in and the magical source released. It took several crystals to clear a single river. He could not continue at this pace, for the crystals were limited along with his power. He needed the people of Solasta to return.

Magnus was slowly healing. Merlin continued his efforts to restore Solasta as he waited for his brother to be well enough to travel through the Kelpie Ring. Once in the mortal realm, Brianna would be able to heal her uncle. Merlin was tempted to question his brother and understand what had happened, but he had to be patient. Magnus was in no state mentally or physically to undergo such questioning. It had been a week and Magnus was finally able to sit up in his bed. Merlin was overjoyed when he walked into his brothers' room to see Magnus with a gentle smile waiting for him to bring a plate of food to break his fast. "I see, brother, you have been able to regain some strength.

I believe you have been prolonging your recovery so that I would continue to wait on you," smirked Merlin, happy to see his brothers' progress. The brothers had been in Solasta for a week while Merlin attempted to repair what he could.

"It is time for us to return to the mortal realm," Merlin told his brother. "I have done all that I can to restore our homeland, but I need our fae family to return and awaken the lands once again. In addition, the food stores that I was able to procure are quickly diminishing." Magnus understood Merlin's concern. If he could only regain his strength, he would have been able to restore all the lands with a simple flick of his wrist. The Ailey family was an ancient bloodline. Magnus was the eldest of the three brothers. He would have been king of the fae if it were not for Stygian. Merlin still did not understand what had transpired after he had left Solasta so many years ago. One day Magnus would regale the family of his misadventure, and Merlin would be there to provide the heroic conclusion.

The following day, Merlin made all the preparations needed for their travel into the mortal realm. Their world had changed, but soon it would be revived. Merlin gathered his brother and they began their journey to Asheboro Keep.

CHAPTER 22

The Prodigal Brother Returns

CAMERON WAS RUSHED to his guest chambers within Asheboro Keep. The battle had lasted only an hour, but the men of the keep felt as though it went on for an eternity. Many were lost, and preparations had begun to collect their fallen to provide them a proper burial. The knights were still stunned from battle and needed tending to. Maximus, once assured all the men were being treated and his services were no longer needed, immediately went to the women's chamber. He hoped all was well and Brianna had awakened from her spell. Maximus reached the chamber door afraid that Merlin's plan did not work. He gently placed his hand on the latch and slowly entered the room.

Taking a steading breath, Maximus walked in to see his two elder daughters seated on the floor with their mother providing much-needed care. Celeste and Aurora were magnificent, but the amount of magic they used had taken its toll on them, and they needed rest. Guinevere assisted Jada with the young women and assured they were comfortable with pillows. Maximus knew his elder daughters would be well, but what about his youngest child? Maximus looked toward the bed. Brianna lay there in a peaceful slumber. Her cheeks were rosy and all seemed well. Maximus did not understand why she had not awakened yet.

The war was over, Stygian returned to Solasta, and the evil horde was no longer able to regenerate. Jada saw the worry in his eyes. She reminded him the entirety of Merlin's scheme. "She will not awaken until her golem has died." Maximus was deep in thought after Jada had revealed what had transpired while he was on the battlefield. "I trust your brother, Maximus. All that he explained and demanded of us has come to success. We defeated the Dark Fae King. We must now wait for Merlin's return and for Brianna to awaken." It seemed an eon for Brianna to rouse from her attachment spell. As each hour ticked by, the family grew more and more anxious. Many thoughts ran through their minds. Perhaps Brianna had been in the enchantment for far too long and now she could not awaken, or Merlin was discovered by Stygian and their golem did not accomplish her task, or the worst thought of all—Merlin was killed, the golem captured, and Stygian now plotting his return to the mortal realm having absorbed Merlin's magic. Jada peered into her husband's eyes, "Maximus, all will be well. Brianna will awaken soon."

After being saved from the molten lava, Cameron was laid in his chambers to rest. He was badly burned and his lungs struggled for breath from the copious amounts of smoke he inhaled during his attempt to escape the horde and Stygian. The keep did their best to make him comfortable but knew if Brianna did not awaken soon there would be no hope of Cameron surviving this injury. His brother, Robert, kept watch over him and would refuse to leave his side when the chambermaids came to relieve him of his duty. Cameron's' body would tense from the pain. His fists would clench and relax sporadically due to the muscles attempting to recover from their exertion. There was no relief for him. Without Brianna's healing powers, Cameron would die from his wounds. Merlin's enchanted armor was able to keep Cameron from mortal wounds but could not save him from the burns he sustained from Stygian's ball of fire.

A sennight had passed and Brianna had not awakened. Merlin had yet to return to Asheboro Keep. Cameron was barely holding onto life. Each passing day he showed no improvement. His condition was continuing to deteriorate. His brother kept vigil and cared for Cameron. Teas and tinctures were made to soothe Cameron's pain, but he was beginning to fade. Jada would check in on the young Laird every morning to change his bandages, provide him a fresh dressing, and apply the salves Brianna had always used.

There was no improvement. Jada's heart broke every day when her daughter did not wake. As she refreshed his bandages, Jada would tell the Laird of the day's events, Brianna's current condition. She hoped her words would provide him strength. Each day that passed, Jada saw Cameron slowly slipping away. His breath was becoming shallower. His skin was becoming infected and pale. Brianna needed to awaken.

Finally, on the tenth day after Stygian returned to Solasta, Brianna awoke from the spell. She was famished and weak. As she began to rouse, her eyes fluttered open, and the first person she saw was her beloved father. She smiled a soft grin and lifted her hand to her father's cheek to assure herself that he was not a phantom. His eyes began to well up with tears. His baby was finally awake. Maximus' joy could not be contained. He pulled her into his arms and held her for what seemed an eternity.

Maximus had never left her side. His youngest daughter was willing to sacrifice her happiness, powers, and life to save her realm. He held onto the amulet that contained her magic. The moment she would wake he would transfer them to their rightful owner. He only hoped it was not too late to save Cameron. Maximus rang for the servants. As they entered they were elated to find the young maiden awake. Maximus ordered food and a warm bath for Brianna, followed by a request for his wife to come to the chamber.

The joy within the keep hearing of Brianna's spell being broken was short lived. Cameron had struggled throughout the evening and his breathing became more labored, his body was feverish, and no amount of cooling salves would break it. Jada and Guinevere kept constant vigil. They could not understand how he had so many infections. They had been so diligent in cleaning his wounds and providing fresh dressings. It seemed as if all their efforts had no effect. Each time Jada or Guinevere came to cleanse Cameron, his bandages showed that they were changed. Yet the wounds continued to fester.

His younger brother was always attentive, but at times he was a pest and did not allow the women to complete their tasks. Eventually, he was removed from the room by the Ailey brothers and Laird Asheboro to allow the healers to work. They hoped the elixir Merlin had left them during Cameron's sleeping spell would aid in his recovery as it contained Brianna's tears, but it did not. Fever consumed his body and Jada could not control it. His body was shutting down and the infection was spreading throughout. She summoned for cool waters from the enchanted Ring. This would buy her more time. All the Ailey siblings rushed to do as she asked. Using their new found knowledge of portals from Merlin, the Ailey siblings were able to travel to the Ring within minutes. Cameron was in and out of consciousness. Robert looked on as the Ailey family attempted to save his brother. He followed the Ailey siblings to the Ring to provide more assistance in carrying whatever they may need. They saw no harm in having him accompany them.

As Jada waited for her children to return with the enchanted waters, she summoned the chambermaid to bring fresh water from the well. Cameron needed Brianna, but his time was quickly flying by. The chambermaid rushed in with the water and announced the good news. Brianna was awake. "Thank the gods and elder fae," Jada sobbed with relief. Now all would be well. All she needed to do was keep Cameron alive for Brianna to visit him. She would be weak but able to extend his life. As Jada spoke to the chambermaid, Cameron's body began to convulse uncontrollably while he gasped for air. Terror took hold of Jada. "Quickly, we need Brianna here now!" Jada yelled to the chambermaid. The young maid ran as fast as her legs could take her to Brianna's room. Maximus was completing the transfer of Brianna's powers to her when the maid burst into the room.

"Brianna is needed, it is urgent. Laird Cedar-Kellen is dying as we speak!" Maximus had not spoken of Cameron as he was more concerned with her wellbeing. Brianna looked at her in utter shock. "What has happened?" Maximus did not have time to explain. "I will explain all in due course but first we must save the Laird. Can you walk, my dear child?" Brianna was very weak and attempted to move her legs but they felt as if they were lead weights. Her eyes reflected the terror she felt. Her father scooped Brianna into his arms and rushed to the Lairds' chamber.

Brianna prayed to the fae Elders, hoping they would arrive in time. Maximus slammed into the Lairds' door and ran to his bed. Jada was sobbing. "It is too late. He is gone. I did all I could do but I could not stop his fever or the convulsions." Maximus lowered Brianna to her feet. He continued to hold her to provide her the much needed support. Her handsome, adventurous Laird, laid in his bed beaten, broken, and marred. What had they done to her love? While she laid in a suspended sleep her betrothed fought a battle that was unbeatable.

Maximus helped her sit on the bed next to Cameron. In that instant the Ailey siblings walked in with Robert. Robert, seeing the hysteria, realized his brother had passed from his wounds. He dropped the two pails of enchanted water he was carrying and fell to his knees. Celeste and Aurora were in utter shock. First in seeing their sister awake and second that the young Laird had succumbed to his injuries. Brianna could not accept this fate. They all had sacrificed too much for it to end in this manner.

"Bring me pomegranate wine." Brianna yelled to the room. No one moved as they were still in shock. "BRING IT!" she commanded and sent the chambermaid who had followed them to retrieve it. She then directed her attention to her family members. "Is this water from the Kelpie Ring?" River and Rune nodded with a somber stance. "Bring me the pails." Brianna was still not strong enough to stand but was able to draw magic from the waters to strengthen her healing powers. Once the wine arrived, she drank a glass and began to scan Cameron's body with her mind. She would not believe his life had ended until she felt his soul no longer resided within his body.

There it was, a small spark. His heart barely beating and his breath no more than a whisper. He was alive. Brianna began to work quickly. Using the magic from the waters, Brianna began to massage Cameron's wounds with her hands. Slowly his skin began to heal. The blisters and burns subsided. His skin was renewing. Brianna's hands glowed from her magic and she quickly worked on every portion of his chest that had refused to heal. The more Brianna used the water, the darker it grew. It was as if she was pulling the maladies from his body. She was beginning to grow weak from her work. Jada was becoming worried that Brianna would kill herself in attempting to save the Laird.

"More wine," Brianna yelled. She drank another glass. The first bucket of enchanted water was now completely black. Maximus removed it from Brianna's side and brought a second to her. Before she used its waters to continue healing Cameron, she drank from it as well. Brianna knew she would not be able to continue for much longer, but the waters would provide enough magic for her to heal Cameron. "Mix a glass of the wine with the water and set it aside for the both of us," she spoke to her mother. Jada did as Brianna asked and set aside the mixture for the couple.

Brianna slowly began to feel Cameron's heart begin beating stronger, his breathing deeper. She was powerful but could not heal all of the injuries. His skin had faint marks from his burns. His handsome face was restored with a patch of skin beneath his left eye jagged from the slash of a sword. Brianna was fading quickly. Color was returning to Cameron's cheeks. Everyone in the room could not believe their eyes. Cameron was returning to the land of the living. Brianna needed more water from the Kelpie Ring. Her brothers placed the pails they carried by her side. Maximus could see his daughter was weakening. She would not stop until she saw her love begin to stir. Then she would be satisfied. Brianna gave Cameron's' body one last wash from the fresh water her brothers gave her. She then asked for the water and wine mixture.

Cameron's external wounds were healed but he still needed his internal injuries to recover. Brianna prayed to the Elders, asking for their strength as she slowly dripped the wine into his dry chapped lips. Brianna was becoming dizzy from all her work, and the cup was beginning to slip from her hands. Jada quickly summoned her elder daughters to assist their sister. Celeste and Aurora held their sister as Jada began to slowly administer the wine to Cameron. His eyes began to move, and Brianna saw his long eyelashes flutter ever so gently. She had saved her love. She could now rest. The moment Cameron was able to open his eyes, Brianna fainted into her sister's arms.

Merlin and Magnus Arrive at Asheboro Keep

To Merlin it seemed an eternity had passed since he left the mortal realm and entered Solasta. Over the last 10 days, he had assured Solasta was no longer under Stygian's evil rule. The dark king now lay in a coffin made of stone, buried under the rubble of his castle. The golem had completed her task. It broke his heart to see her sacrifice, but it was a necessary evil to assure Solasta's future. Now his brother, Magnus, would reunite with the family and the healing of both realms could begin.

The journey to the keep typically would only be a half day journey on foot. Due to Magnus not being completely recovered from his imprisonment, the journey was slow and laborious. Over the course of two days, the brothers finally reached their destination, Asheboro Keep.

Relief washed over Merlin as he saw the keep still standing. The Ailey family truly were miraculous. Brianna for her sacrifice, Celeste and Aurora for their unwavering trust and precision. The Ailey men standing among their fellow fae to defend their home. King Arthur and his knights to hold off the horde long enough, while he attempted to stop Stygian.

As the men grew closer to the keep, Magnus began to shake. Concerned, Merlin asked "Are you well, brother?" Magnus did not know how to explain how he had parted the family. He and Maximus were not on good terms. They may not be greeted with the warmest of welcomes.

Merlin knocked on the portcullis door. One of the knights from the inner bailey answered their call. "We seek an audience with the Laird and King. Please notify them Merlin has returned from Solasta." The knight swiftly left the door to convey the message. Merlin waited patiently for the knight to return. "Magnus, what is ailing you? We are safe and welcome here. There is no need to fear these people." Magnus shook his head, "You do not understand, dear brother, what I have done. Maximus will never forgive my transgressions." Merlin was about to speak when the portcullis door began to open. Immediately Maximus and King Arthur greeted the pair at the door. All were in good spirits, except for Magnus.

At first Maximus did not recognize his younger brother and wondered who the unfortunate fae was. Merlin proceeded to greet the knights and the rest of the family within the keep. The men were then escorted to the banquet hall for a hearty meal. "Regale us Merlin, of your adventure. What dangers did you face and how did our enemy come to his end?" The hall grew silent as they awaited with bated breath to hear of Merlin's triumphant feats. Merlin began his tale of cunning and stealth. How he nearly was overtaken by Stygian's minions and relished in their demise. Merlin's tone became somber as he spoke of the golem and her sacrifice to save both the fae and mortal realm.

The hall raised their goblets to the fallen golem to commemorate her heroic martyrdom. Merlin then came to explain his guest. "A long-lost brother was imprisoned within Stygian's castle. He was found starved in a damp and dirty cell. I introduce to you my brother, Magnus." The hall roared with cheers and congratulations. No one noticed Maximus's reaction except for Merlin. Once the meal was over he would bring his brothers together and hopefully understand what caused the tension between the siblings. Maximus slowly stood and left the hall quietly. He would not disrupt the jubilation, as there should be a celebration of the realms being freed from the evil fae king.

The feast continued into the late hours of the evening, and Merlin was growing weary. "Come Magnus, let us find our family and have some much-needed rest." Magnus had sat throughout the entire dinner fretting about this moment. How would he explain to Maximus what had happened; how would he ever be forgiven for his actions; he could not be redeemed in the eyes of the fae world. "Merlin, before we join our family, I must first explain myself and the fear that is currently gripping me." Merlin looked at his brother and gently guided him to the keep's library. They sat for a long time before Magnus had the courage to begin his tale.

"My dear brother, the day you disappeared from Solasta, the family thought you had died after the skirmish between you and Stygian. We were at a loss. How could our beloved brother be gone? Maximus, as he always did, rallied the family and devised a plan to search for your remains. Mother and Father pleaded with him to not pursue it. They had already lost one son; they did not want to lose another. They knew it would only be a matter of time before Stygian would come to rise and destroy all of our world. In the midst of your disappearance and Maximus' want for revenge, I was pushed aside, ignored. It was no excuse other than my own immaturity. I began to grow angry with our family. I thought to myself, if they do not want to pay attention to me, then I will make them. Stygian had just come into power. He was bribing the most affluent families to align with him. Our parents refused his generous offers and paid the highest price for their disobedience."

Merlin took in a steadying breath. He knew what Magnus had done. He had made an alliance with the Dark Fae King in hopes of saving himself. "I see," Merlin said. Magnus continued to explain the alliance he made with Stygian. He was Stygian's second in command. He took part in the beatings, humiliation, and killing of his fellow villagers.

"In my own mind, I hoped our parents would have noticed how I was protecting them from harm, but all I did was bring shame and dishonor to our name." Merlin then asked, "How did you come to be imprisoned and not killed by the evil fae?"

"The last order I was given by Stygian before my imprisonment was to seek out my family line and have them all murdered as traitors. He knew our family was the oldest bloodline. Our powers surpassed all others. If he was able to absorb our magic, he would have been unstoppable. I denied his request. I would not spill my familial blood for his kingdom. I reminded him of our alliance. I would only join his ranks and do his bidding as long as my family would remain unharmed. I truly went in with the best of intentions, even though our family did not see it in such a manner. My naivete got the best of me. I actually thought Stygian would keep his word. I wanted to be the hero."

Merlin still did not understand why his brother was not simply killed for his blatant refusal. "Brother, that still does not explain why you were not simply slain." With tears in his eyes, he looked at Merlin. "I promised him an heir from our bloodline. I was a coward. Jada had recently given birth to Brianna. In a blood ceremony, I linked our blood to a Jasper stone. Stygian did not know of the old ways.

He believed the ceremony would tie him to the youngest Ailey child and provide him the needed power to destroy the Kelpie Ring. He kept the crystal but was not able to access its power without me. Brianna was never in danger, or so I thought. Once Stygian realized what I had done, he became enraged. My powers were locked within it. If he were to kill me, there would have been no way for him to access them. Only our family knew of the sacred spell to shield our powers from others. As punishment, he locked me in the dungeon. Day after day he attempted to extract the magic from the stone. As a last effort to make me acquiesce to his request, he brought our parents to his evil court. Creating a spectacle, I was dragged in, beaten and chained. Our mother screamed; she never lost hope that I would one day return. Stygian explained to them what I had done. Our father smirked, for he knew there was no way to break the spell I had created. This angered Stygian even more."

Merlin could not believe what he was hearing. Magnus continued to recount the last moments of the meeting. The patriarch and matriarch of the Ailey family had been murdered by the Dark Fae King. He could see the turmoil and remorse Magnus felt. His parents were murdered as a way to force him to relinquish his powers, and he did not. Magnus did not know where the stone now resided. He was a fae, but held no power. This was his atonement for all the evil he had caused. He knew Maximus would never forgive his actions. The anguish his brother felt was too much for Merlin. He went to his brother and shared the vision he'd received from the elder fae so many years ago.

Magnus felt the warmth of Merlin's hands on his shoulders. His mind began to flood with images. Merlin spoke barely above a whisper. "I am the seventh son of the seventh son. I was destined to return to save our world. I knew our family would suffer and Stygian would come to power. I knew you would turn your back on us the moment

I left, but I needed you to fulfill your role. If you had not followed your fate our world would have fallen."

Magnus' eyes grew wide. Merlin had known all along. He did not have the details on how the events would unfold, but he knew his leaving would set into motion the rise and fall of the Dark Fae King. Merlin embraced his brother and asked for forgiveness. He could not explain to his family why he needed to disappear without affecting the outcome of their futures. The brothers remained in the library for a few more moments. The Ailey family needed time to heal. They had made the greatest sacrifice of all the fae to save both realms. "Tonight we shall rest. Tomorrow we will face Maximus." Merlin escorted Magnus out of the room and asked a servant girl to help them to their chambers.

For the first time in years, Magnus was at peace. Merlin wept in his chambers for the lost lives of his parents. The brutality his family had to suffer was more than he could bear. He knew his fate and what had to be accomplished but the cost nearly killed him. Solasta would rise again. Merlin would assure no other power would ever keep him from his family ever again.

CHAPTER 23

New Beginnings

THE REVELERS WOKE up the next morning tired and hungover. The keep no longer had a sense of impending doom. The realms had been saved. It was now time for some much-needed rest. Laird Asheboro had been generous throughout this time. He was hosting the King and his new bride, fighting a war, and allowing the Laird of Cedar-Kellen to stay as an honored guest while he recovered from his injuries. All was well again. The villagers slowly returned to their homes in Haven. Their fields were destroyed, livestock lost, and homes turned to rubble. The daunting task of caring for the dead and rebuilding in the mortal realm or Solasta was on every fae's mind.

Many of the fae families feared if they left the mortal realm they would be trapped once again by the Kelpie Ring. Maximus knew he needed to help lead his village but with the arrival of Magnus, he was not himself. He needed time to process his traitor of a brother's arrival; the fact that Solasta was once again safe for them to return; and the life he had built in Haven Village.

King Arthur and Guinevere stayed an additional fortnight after the battle to assure Asheboro Keep was back in working order. Laird Cedar-Kellen was well enough to return to his own lands, leaving the keep the same day King Arthur and his bride departed. Before his departure, Cameron promised to return to properly ask for Brianna's hand in marriage.

Merlin consulted with the King as he left, reassuring Arthur he would return to his royal court in Camelot once all was settled with his family and Solasta. All that remained was the matter of the Kelpie Ring and the future of Solasta. Merlin knew that his brothers would not, without force, be in each other's presence. His attempts of a family reconciliation had failed miserably over the last several days. In hopes of maintaining cordiality between the brothers, Merlin invited Laird Asheboro to a village meeting, in addition to Laird Cedar-Kellen to attend now that he was back at Asheboro Keep. The scene was set, and Merlin prayed to the Elders things would go smoothly.

Village Meeting

A month had passed and finally Haven Village was able to hold their village meeting. All the families were asked to

attend to discuss the future plans of their lands in Solasta. Merlin led the meeting with Maximus seated to his right and Magnus to his left. "Thank you all for attending this evening. We have much to announce and discuss. We have had a harrowing year thus far. Stygian usurping the fae thrown; his devious plan to destroy the mortal world. Our lands were plundered and families torn apart. Even though there is much to mourn, we also have much to celebrate. Solasta has been freed from the darkness. The fae and mortal realm are once again unified with our gracious friend, Laird Asheboro. One must not forget the betrothal of our dear Lady Brianna and Laird Cedar-Kellen. They have fought for our survival, risked their very own happiness, to assure our worlds would not be destroyed."

The first order of business Merlin wanted to address was the Kelpie Ring and Solasta. The enchantment he placed on the Ring would allow for free movement between the realms. He did warn the villagers that the enchantment was intended for those who followed the Dark Fae King to be entrapped within the fae realm and never to reenter the mortal world. The villagers applauded with excitement. The fear of the darkness returning was quickly dispelled. Merlin continued to elaborate on the state of Solasta.

"Before I returned to Asheboro Keep, I used the crystals from Stygian's cloak to restore portions of our land. Though my powers are strong, they were not able to undo all that Stygian had destroyed. I returned hoping you would continue the rebuilding of our once-beautiful realm. The waters are clean and the forests returned. All that is missing are its people to cultivate the land and bring life to it once more. I know this decision should not be made in haste and perhaps families will decide to live in both realms."

Merlin continued to speak with the villagers and answered their questions. Before Solasta could be occupied once more, the villagers needed to select a new Fae King or Queen. The previous royal line had been assassinated by Stygian and his minions. No one from the elder line remained. "How are we to select a new leader, when the royal line has been eradicated?" spoke a villager. "We do not have any next of kin," said another. Merlin pondered their inquiries. They were correct that there was no fae who held the elder bloodline that they were aware of.

Whoever was to be the next fae leader needed to be just, honorable, and uphold the balance between good and evil. "We will request an audience with the King," Merlin said. "He holds Excalibur. If the King will grant us this audience, we will be able to use Excalibur to select our next King or Queen." Magnus looked bewildered about how a sword could designate a King or Queen. "Excalibur can only be wielded by the true King of England and the rightful heir. If he were to use Excalibur to select our next leader, the sword would reveal if the fae we selected would be a wise and fair leader." The villagers spoke among themselves. Maximus was the first to speak. "If it is true what you say, brother, let us hold a tournament with a member from each household being represented. Our top four competitors will then see the King."

The hall roared with cheers from the villagers. A fete would be perfect to celebrate their new beginnings. "Are we in agreement?" asked Merlin.

The villagers replied with a resounding "Yea!" All the young men of the village became eager to showcase their prowess. The tournament would not be for the faint of heart. There would be events of strength, cunning, and accuracy.

There was excitement in the air, and the villagers were finally able to see a future for Solasta. Before the village meeting could be adjourned, Maximus stood to address everyone. "In the midst of darkness there has always been light. Before the darkness arrived at Asheboro Keep, we had a young couple brought together by the fates." Maximus proceeded to ask Brianna and Cameron to join him at the front of the hall. "Our dear Brianna saved a stranger who in turn saved our world. A chance meeting with only a brooch and tartan as gifts. A serendipitous invitation sent to a neighboring clan that led to our two lovers to reunite. Their love will be a story for the ages. This very evening I announce to you the betrothal of Laird Cedar-Kellen and Lady Brianna Sky Ailey! Join me with a goblet of pomegranate wine and toast to the future Laird and Lady Cedar-Kellen." The roar of cheers was deafening as goblets were raised to celebrate the newly betrothed couple. As the meeting ended, families visited the couple to express their well wishes. All was well in the Scottish Highlands.

CHAPTER 24

The Hunt

A FORTNIGHT HAD passed since the villagers held their meeting. The moment the decision was made to hold a tournament, Merlin sent word to Arthur. Once the future of Solasta was secured, he would return to Camelot and Arthur's court. The village was again alive with laughter and business. As the preparations for the tournament were underway, Cameron and Brianna were planning their handfasting ceremony.

As part of the tournament, they would end the festivities with their wedding. Maximus met with the couple; as a gift they were bequeathed land within Solasta. It was Brianna's home and she was to do as she wished with the property.

Knowing they would not be able to live in Solasta, they were first confused with the patriarch's generous gift. "Brianna, Solasta will forever be a part of you. You may not be able to live in your former home, but you will be able to use it for its amazing gifts. If you recall, before our escape, I gave each of my children a small box of earth."

"Yes, it remains safely with my personal belongings," Brianna stated.

"Good, it will serve you well in the future. Assure that it always remains near you."

Realization began to dawn. Brianna would be able to grow her herbs and have a working cottage to process her salves. Maximus continued, "Your brothers have decided to settle in Solasta and be a part of its rebuilding. They will build you a small cottage with a garden and orchard." Maximus then proceeded to hand her a small golden key. "Insert this key into any door in your new home here and it will instantly transport you to your cottage in Solasta as long as you maintain your small box of earth." Cameron's eyes grew wide as he learned of this new-found magic.

"How is this possible?" he asked.

"With the help of Merlin, we were able to create an enchantment to guarantee your safety and that of Brianna. Our powers are blessings from the elder fae, but not all mortals are as willing to accept us as you and Laird Asheboro have been. If you are ever in danger use the key to escape into our realm. This shall be a secret among us and no one else. If the key and earth were to fall into the wrong hands, Solasta may once again be at risk."

Brianna embraced her father, thanking him for his generosity. "There is still more," Maximus told the couple. The Ailey brothers walked into the small chamber carrying a beautifully carved trunk with elaborate designs of thistles and roses. The side panels told the story of their first encounter, depicting Cameron hunting for the stag and Brianna coming to his aid. Inside the ornate trunk was Brianna's trousseau. As she opened the chest, she saw it contained fine silks from her mother's special stores, delicate lace linens, and two gorgeous gowns: one made of her future clan's tartan and the other a royal purple to match her lavender eyes. Hidden underneath the gowns was a beautifully embroidered swaddling blanket with a matching gown.

Brianna's eyes welled with tears of joy. She did not know how she was so deserving of such treasures. Within a sennight, she would be a wife living in a strange land and home. She looked into Cameron's eyes. He saw the fear hidden behind her seductive lavender eyes. "Do not worry, my love. You will be loved by all at Cedar-Kellen just as you are here. You won the hearts of my people the day you saved my life." She took in a steadying breath. Cameron lifted her hand gently to his lips, enjoying the wonderful fragrance of roses and lavender before placing a gentle kiss upon it. "Until tomorrow, my lady." Cameron left the family to attend to his men.

Tents began to sprawl all over the land as visiting guests from Clan Cedar-Kellen arrived. Knights throughout the realm joined the festivities to take part in a ceremonial jousting tourney. Asheboro Keep was once again honored to receive word that King Arthur and his knights would once again be joining them to enjoy the fete and bless the marriage of Laird Cedar-Kellen and Lady Brianna. The fields were being prepared, the kitchens were brimming with delicacies, and the contestants were ready for action.

Finally, the day for the opening ceremonies arrived. Laird Asheboro and his famous drummer opened the tourney to all the guests. Tables lined the lawn for everyone to enjoy a few refreshments before the jousting. King Arthur sat on a dais with Laird Asheboro to watch over the festivities. Guests made their way to the jousting field where they could hear the clashing of titans as swords and lances collided.

Being the honored guest, King Arthur selected a Queen of the Tourney to bless her favored contestant in each event. As he made his rounds, he could not deny Brianna the honor. If it were not for her trust in Merlin and selflessness they may all have perished in the battle.

Arthur approached Brianna. "My fair lady, I humbly ask you to be our Queen of the Tourney." Brianna, embarrassed by the attention, curtsied to the King. "You honor me, Your Highness," and accepted his five tokens to be given to her favored champion. Brianna was accompanied by Laird Cedar-Kellen to the dais and enjoyed the parade of knights entering the jousting tournament. Each knight presented their shields and lances with their family banners being displayed. Brianna could not help but admire the beautiful coats of arm and the vibrant colors on display. Each knight circled the jousting field holding a rose.

The village women swooned with the chivalry on display. As the knights made their rounds, they would throw their rose to a maiden they deemed to be the fairest in the land. The last knight to present himself was Sir Lancelot. He paraded the field to find a maiden but could not find one that matched Brianna's beauty. He returned to the dais and presented his rose, "My fair lady, it seems that I have been enamored by your beauty. Would you accept my rose?" Brianna took a moment and looked at her betrothed and the King. "Thank you, my good Knight. I wish you well in the tourney."

She carefully accepted his rose and returned to her chair. Something about the knight made her uneasy, but she could not say why. Laird Asheboro then rose and addressed the crowd. Before the jousting could begin, Brianna needed to select her champion. The Laird turned to Brianna and asked who she would choose as her favored knight. With the memory of her rescue and the bravery she witnessed, Brianna chose Sir Galahad as her champion. She gently tied her token of a silk embroidered handkerchief to his lance and wished him well.

Once Brianna returned to her chair, the tournament began. The event was invigorating. The villagers had never seen such a spectacle and relished every moment. The tournament was to last for four days to allow all the contestants the opportunity to rest if they were to compete in more than one event. Brianna watched in anticipation as Sir Galahad won each of his rounds. The sun was beginning to set and the final match was ready to begin, Sir Galahad against Sir Lancelot. Brianna looked at her love and asked which he believed would win. "Sir Lancelot is cunning, but Sir Galahad has heart. I believe you chose well, my love; your champion will win today's event."

The rules were simple. The knights had three passes to unseat their opponent. If neither was successful, they would jump from their horses and spar until one of the knight took a knee.

The drummer announced the beginning of the first pass. The crowd held their breath in anticipation of the first blow. The horses raced to the other end of the field as their respective knights lowered their lances. Sir Galahad was only a second slower than Sir Lancelot in hitting his target. Neither knight fell from his horse. A point was granted to Sir Lancelot for a broken lance on his opponent. The knights readied themselves once again. The drum rolled to announce the next round. The flag was dropped, and this time Sir Galahad was the first to leave his post and position his lance on his target. Sir Lancelot was almost unseated, but he held on.

Sir Galahad gained a point for his broken lance. The men were now on their last pass. If neither could be unseated, it would come down to a sparring match. The crowd began to cheer for Brianna's champion, invigorating the knight. The drum began to roll again as the knights prepared for their last pass. Sir Lancelot, frustrated with his abilities, missed the flag to leave his post. Sir Galahad was the first to leave and hit his target. Lancelot was hit with such force he fell from his horse.

The crowd grew wild and cheered for the jousting champion. Both knights walked to the dais and bowed to their King. "Well done, gentlemen. You have displayed both bravery and skill. You have honored and represented Camelot well." King Arthur applauded his knights and rewarded Sir Galahad with a small pouch of gold.

The jousting fields began to empty as everyone prepared for the evening libations and entertainment. A caravan of minstrels were commissioned to entertain the keep during the tournament. They wowed the revelers with their acrobatics and sword swallowing. The singers and storytellers sang of King Arthur and his knights. The evenings were magical as new stories unfolded of distant lands with exotic animals and spices. As the entertainment ended, the villagers made their way home to prepare for the next day's events of archery and the caber toss.

The following three days flew by as fast as a hummingbird searching for nectar. River, the eldest of the Ailey brothers, won both his events of Archery and the Caber Toss. The reigning champion, Brock, stole the show with his prowess in the stone put. After five rounds, no one could beat his distance.

There were now two candidates to be the next ruler of Solasta. No maiden had attempted any of the events to join their ranks. This saddened Brianna, for she would have loved a Queen to rule her home. One with a heart for the people, intellect to withstand treacherous dealings, and a love for both the fae and mortal realms. A bridge between the realms to bring a new age of peace. But alas, it would not be.

The last day of the tourney was upon them. The following day, Brianna and Cameron would be married and she would have her very own fairytale. Today's event was the stag hunt. There were five teams. The first two teams were led by Rune and Ronan, Brianna's older brothers; followed by Echo and his fast flying fae; the last two groups to join the hunt were from obscure families but held respect within Asheboro Keep. Arthur's drummer announced the beginning of the hunt and the fae were off.

The excitement in the air was electrifying. The remaining villagers kept watch and sent runners to keep everyone informed of the hunt's progress. The first team to return with a stag would win the event, with the captain being the last candidate to become the King of Solasta. As Arthur was in residence, the wedding was to be held at Asheboro keep. An hour passed before the first runner returned to the village fete to report his findings. The young runner, exhausted, was welcomed with a goblet of water before he regaled the villagers of the hunt. The hunting party of Captain Echo was in hot pursuit of a stag and had a near miss in capturing his prize. Rune was the second group in the lead. The other three groups had yet to be able to find a stag to hunt. Once the village had their fill of the news, they sent another runner to continue to watch.

As the men of the village awaited for the results of the stag hunt, the women busied themselves preparing for the wedding. Asheboro keep was transformed into a living garden with heather, lavender, and roses adorning the archway and chapel. Laird Asheboro was a gracious host and having the King in residence would not allow Cameron and Brianna to be wed elsewhere.

Jada had just finished sewing Brianna's wedding gown, placing the finishing touches. It was a beautiful, red-silk brocade design of roses with gold accents. The collar and hem were lined with ermine and a delicate gold chain would accentuate Brianna's slender waist.

To complete the wedding outfit, Brianna's sisters and mother worked tirelessly to embroider Brianna's golden veil with red roses and an intricate filigree design. "My love, visit with me in my chamber," Jada called to her youngest daughter. The Ailey women beamed at Brianna as they slowly revealed their gift. Brianna had no words for the beauty she was witnessing. Tears began to well as she walked to her mother and sisters.

"My sweet child, a gown befitting a queen. You are now part of both worlds. May this small token be a beacon of strength as you enter into the new role of wife." Not wanting to cry herself, Jada quickly asked Brianna, "Please go, try on your new gown to assure there are no adjustments needed." The weight of the brocade fabric brought comfort to Brianna as her mother began to lace the dress into place. It fit like a glove. The soft ermine lining the collar caressed her milky white skin and gave her a regal stance. Celeste and Aurora looked in awe as their little sister transformed from a beautiful young maiden into a strong and regal woman.

"Cameron—I mean Laird Cedar-Kellen—will not know what to do with himself," giggled Celeste.

"You are truly a vision, Brianna," Aurora chimed. Brianna relished the moment for a minute longer before removing the gown.

As was tradition the day before the wedding, Brianna and Cameron were kept from each other. They each had their entourage to assure the couple would not meet. This of course was difficult with the fete still in full swing and the hunt in progress.

Echo and his men were in hot pursuit of a stag in the middle of the woods. They finally were able to find an area to position themselves around a clearing to wait for him to emerge. Their bodies were shaking from exhaustion and beads of sweat continued to race down their backs. Echo kept watch and signaled his men to stay alert.

Rune and his men had been tracking a stag of their own when they happened upon Echo. "Damn the gods,"

Echo cursed his luck. They now would have to be faster than ever to assure they were the first to down the animal. There was a light rustle in the clearing and a gentle breeze made its way through the men. Slowly the stag made his way to the center of the clearing. He knew there were men hunting him but could not sense their location.

The stag stared into the depths of the forest. His muscles tensed and twitched as he continued to walk through the clearing. The hunting parties prepared their arrows, praying to the fae Elders to make their them fly true. Rune held his breath as he pulled his arrow back, ready to be released. He finally saw the stag perfectly placed in the center of the clearing. It seemed as if the animal were attempting to see into the forest and locate his hunters. Rune sent up a small fae blessing and unleashed his arrow. The whisper of the arrow sung through the air as it made its way toward the stag's jugular.

Rune saw his arrow moving perfectly toward its target. Right before it landed its mark, another arrow from the opposite direction swooshed by and knocked his arrow out of the way. A second arrow followed, felling the stag. A cacophony of noise broke the silence of the clearing. Echo and his fae men had won! The cheers followed them as they ran toward the stag to collect their prize.

Rune cursed the Elders for such foul luck. At least his older brother River had won both his events. This at least guaranteed an Ailey family member would be represented for the selection.

CHAPTER 25

Two Worlds Become One

ECHO AND HIS fast-flying fairies made it back to the village before the runner could reach the fete to announce the winner of the hunt. The crowd cheered as they saw Echo arrive with the stag over his shoulders. He quickly proceeded to the raised dais and presented his prize to Laird Asheboro and the King. "Well done, young Echo. You are our last champion for the selection." Brianna presented Echo with one of the favors the King had bestowed upon her.

As she walked up to Echo, Brianna felt uneasy, as if something were amiss. Echo had never harmed her or her family. He was always charming, even though he had his moments of questionable behavior. Once upon a time, she even fancied him as a future husband. She gently placed the token into his hand as if she were afraid to touch his skin.

Echo noticed the slight tremor he brought to Brianna's demeanor. "Fear me not, sweet lass. I would not dare harm the future Lady of Cedar-Kellen," he held her hand for longer than she felt appropriate and placed an unwanted kiss upon it. "Thank you, Echo, for your kind sentiments, but please refrain from such liberties," Brianna replied. Cameron came to her side immediately. King Arthur saw the exchange among the trio and also joined the group. Echo immediately stepped away and bowed to the King. His demeanor changed as if to charm the King. The King knew what Echo was attempting. "Remember, young Echo, Excalibur knows all and only selects those that are of a chivalrous heart. You may rise and join your hunting party. They have much to celebrate." The fae rose and joined his men.

The remaining trio knew Echo would not be the next Fae King. His arrogance alone disqualified him. Excalibur would select well from the remaining champions. As the couple began to stroll together throughout the fete, they completely forgot they were not to see each other before the wedding. Brianna stopped suddenly with the thought and Cameron knew exactly what was on her mind. "Do not fear the old superstitions. We are not ruled by the whims of the wind. Our worlds have come together. Nothing will separate our bond, not even presumptuous fae men." Brianna smiled and admonished him for his words. "We are fae and our Elders in the heavens watch over us. I do not want to lose favor with them."

Not wanting to relinquish her hand, he slowly walked to where Jada was standing giving him the evil eye for tempting the fates. "I return you to your chaperone saved from another rogue." Brianna could not contain herself and laughed as she looked at her mother.

"I will pray to the Elders, mother, for forgiveness. We shall remain apart for the rest of the evening and wait with anticipation for when we are able to be together again." Jada could not stay angry at the pair. They were enamored with each other.

Jada insisted that Brianna go immediately home, but Brianna would not leave the festival so early. She wanted to hear the evening legends and watch the acrobats once more. The fete was raucous this evening with revelers deep into their wine and the court jesters entertaining the masses. The next morning would be the beginning of her new life. Brianna decided after an hour of entertainment she had her fill and was ready to return home.

Cameron admired his future wife from afar. He memorized the soft curve of her face, the glow in her eyes, and the way she would giggle with the other maidens. The awe in her eyes as she was watching the acrobats and the ravenous applause she would bestow upon them. His clansmen came to him and offered some honeyed mead. He thanked them for the gesture but declined. Once Brianna left the fete, he returned to his guest chamber within Asheboro Keep.

Both struggled to fall asleep, anxious and excited for the next day's festivities. Brianna and Cameron were able to finally find some rest as the sun was beginning to rise.

The dawn made the blades of grass glycine with the morning dew. Rays of sunshine created dancing shadows as it made its climb through the sky. The keep was prepared for the nuptials, beautifully adorned with red roses and heather. The servants busied themselves placing the final touches on the food and desserts.

The fae and villagers gathered in the chapel waiting for the ceremony to begin. The men looked dashing in their kilts. Cameron awaited Brianna's arrival, standing at the altar along with his brother Robert. Maximus waited at the chapel entrance to escort his youngest daughter to her soon-to-be husband. In the years he was held captive, he never dreamed that he would have the honor of walking Brianna down the aisle to her future husband.

The future of Solasta was now secure. He could rest peacefully knowing that he was able to save Solasta and bring the fae and mortal realms together once again. She finally arrived. Brianna was radiant in her dark-red gown embellished with gold and a fur collar. Celeste and Aurora lead the procession to the altar, each sister holding a small bouquet of roses and wearing gowns made of their husband's tartan. "Are you ready, my love?" Maximus looked at his daughter.

"Yes, with all my heart," Brianna responded.

They took a deep breath and began their walk to meet the groom. Cameron was stunned by the beautiful maiden making her way toward him. She looked ravishing in her red gown. Her gorgeous raven hair cascaded down her back and neck in soft curls with a portion pinned in an elaborate braid.

His mother's brooch was placed in the braid to hold it in place. He did not know how he'd been so blessed but thanked the gods for his good fortune. Brianna felt the same as she slowly made her way to her future husband. He stood waiting for her, strong and sleek. His kilt and stark white shirt made him an impressive sight to behold, his fiery red hair tamed for the day, neatly tied back with his piercing emerald eyes watching her every move. *Finally*, she thought to herself. Her father placed Brianna's hand in Cameron's and kissed her softly on the cheek before relinquishing his daughter to her husband to be.

The ceremony combined both the fae and Scottish traditions to symbolize not only the marriage of the bride and groom but of the culmination of two worlds. The guests roared with cheers as the couple sealed their marriage with a kiss. The marriage celebration began with a troop of minstrels and dancers in honor of Laird and Lady Cedar-Kellen.

The couple sat at the head table watching their guests feast upon pheasant, venison, and dried fruit with cheeses. The pomegranate wine flowed freely, allowing many shy young men the courage to ask young maidens to dance. Cameron rose from his seat and extended his hand to Brianna.

The clarsach began to play a slow melodious tune accompanied by a bodhran. Brianna felt as if she were swept away into another realm where only she and Cameron existed. They danced as one and the party guests cleared the floor to honor their first dance as husband and wife. As the evening continued, Brianna began to grow tired and wished to leave the party. She simply wanted to be in her husbands' strong arms and drift off to sleep. Before they could retire for the evening, there was one last matter to address. The selection of the next fae king of Solasta.

Arthur called the party to attention and requested the four champions to kneel before him. Brianna and Cameron looked on in anticipation. Maximus and Jada prayed to the Elders that a noble king would be chosen from the lot. Sir Galahad, even though he was not a fae, was given the honor to join the champions. He was accompanied by Echo, River, and Wolfsbane. All four men knelt in front of the king and waited for Excalibur to make its choice. The guests held their breath with anticipation. Soon the next fae king would be revealed.

Arthur stood in front of Echo and presented Excalibur. Echo attempted to lift the sword but it was too heavy. Echo attempted once again to lift the sword from Arthurs' hands, but it would not move. Furious, Echo stormed out of the banquet hall. "So it seems Excalibur has deemed Echo inadequate to the task of Fae King. Perhaps Wolfsbane will have better luck," exclaimed Arthur. The king stood in front of Wolfsbane and presented Excalibur. The fae attempted to lift the sword from the king's hands but it would not move. Once again Excalibur was too heavy to lift.

The crowd began to murmur. Two fae men had been rejected by Excalibur. Perhaps it was meant for the Ailey family to inherit the royal line. Arthur presented River with the sword. He attempted to lift the sword but was not able to lift it more than half an inch from Arthur's hands. Arthur looked at Merlin in wonder.

"How is this possible for him to have some strength to move the sword but not carry it?" Merlin paused for a moment before he answered.

"Remember, Arthur, the sword seeks out those who are pure of heart, have displayed courage, and do not seek power. Each champion thus far has held at least two of the traits but not all three. Perhaps our young River has all three but the sword has not decided if he is the next rightful heir." Arthur accepted this answer and moved to Sir Galahad.

Once again the sword would not move from Arthurs' hand. The wedding guests began to whisper. How could it be that no champion was worthy to rule? River was the closest, but yet not chosen. The entire hall was astounded by the results. Why did Excalibur not select the next Fae King? Merlin then addressed the banquet hall. "It seems Excalibur has not selected a new King to govern Solasta. Perhaps he may believe we should have a Queen to rule our realm? We will hold a council meeting to see how we will proceed. Until then we will continue with our council leaders."

The guests were silent for a moment and there seemed to be some unrest, but the majority accepted Merlin's decision. The only person who voiced his anger was Echo, who had been sulking in a corner. "The Ailey family have been in power for far too long.

Their ties are now with the mortal world. How are they allowed to continue as our ruling family? Brianna is now tied to these people. The fae will suffer for this alliance. We will never be free of them now. I am the rightful successor to the Solastian throne. I am Stygian's cousin.

"He may have been an evil tyrannical fae with a lust for torture and blood, but he was the last Solastian king with no heir. The throne should be passed down to me." A few of the fae villagers were shocked to learn Echo was kin to Stygian and were glad he was not selected. This enraged Echo even more. He left the celebration with his small entourage to drink away his sorrows.

To break the tension among the guests, Arthur signaled for the musicians to play a jig for all to dance. Cameron pulled Brianna onto the floor, twirling her around. Her melodious laughter was contagious. Soon everyone at the reception was once again in good spirits. The drinking and dancing lasted until the wee hours of the morning.

Before the newlyweds left their guests, Cameron had one last request. They never had a traditional courtship or handfasting ceremony. He asked if Arthur could oversee this intimate union with only her parents and Merlin present. Brianna humored her husband and went to fetch her family. They left the banquet hall and stood outside the small chapel. The evening was cool, making Brianna shiver slightly. Arthur stood in front of the couple as they linked their hands.

"May this knot remain tied for as long as love shall last. May the vows you have spoken never grow bitter in your mouths. Hold tight to one another through good times and bad and watch as your strength grows. In the joining of hands and the fashion of a knot, so are your lives now bound, one to another."

As Arthur spoke the words, he carefully wrapped Clan Cedar-Kellen's tartan around the couple's hands. Arthur stuck Excalibur into the ground underneath their love knot. They looked lovingly into each other's eyes and sealed their bond with a kiss. To thank the King, both Brianna and Cameron pledged their fealty to his court. As Excalibur stood between the couple it began to vibrate and slowly illuminate.

In the shadows, Echo watched as King Arthur performed the intimate ceremony for Brianna and Cameron. What he would do to the both of them if the King were not present. He was ready to spoil their fun when he noticed Excalibur shining in the moonlight in between the couple, as if it were coming to life.

This could not be, thought Echo. *No mortal should be the next ruler of Solasta*. Echo, not wanting to be discovered, slowly moved closer to the group. He could no longer hold his anger. Excalibur did not select him, but it would not select a mortal. Rushing toward Cameron, Echo revealed a small dagger poised to strike Cameron in the heart.

Everything happened in an instant. Brianna thought Echo was attempting to harm her. Quickly she released Cameron's' hand, unraveling the knot. The only weapon she had to defend herself was Excalibur.

Without hesitation Brianna, grabbed the sword and thrust it into Echo's shoulder. She did not want to kill him, simply to stop his attack. Echo grunted with pain as the dagger he held fell from his hands. Merlin quickly froze the fae in place. Arthur called to his knights for assistance. They placed silver shackles on Echo to keep him from escaping and using his powers.

Adrenaline was still coursing through Brianna's veins. She looked as if she were a terrified mouse that had been captured in a trap. The group looked in awe as she continued to hold Excalibur illuminating in her hands. She held the sword to her side and immediately dropped it, realizing she had been able not only to lift it but to wield it. Once the group realized what had transpired, they stood in awe of the young maiden and knelt down.

Brianna looked at both her husband and Merlin with shock. Not wanting to believe her thoughts, Brianna asked "What does this mean?"

Cameron gave her a knowing smile. "It means, my love, you are the Queen of Solasta."

The End

A Note of Thanks

To Joanie Newsome for introducing me to NaNoWriMo and setting me on this journey.

NaNoWriMo for supplying the bare bones for me to explore my love of writing.

To my amazing Editor, Laura. With her dedication and patience, she turned my sow's ear into a silk purse.

To my fabulous Book Cover Artist, Catherine. She was able to take all my OCD ideas and create exactly what I was looking for.

A magnanimous thank you to the authors who provided copious amounts of literature to help navigate the publishing world.

Resources

****www.argyll-bute.gov.uk 2/12/24 online access (handfasting quote)

****Emily Bronte Quote 2/15/24 online access